THE VAULTS
OF THE TITANIC

De Wolff Adventure Series volume 1

BERT E. WISEMAN

DEDICATION

To all my Dutch fans who made my books popular in the
Netherlands. I hope that young people of English speaking
audiences enjoy the books just as much.

"Have I not commanded you? Be strong and
courageous. Do not be afraid; do not be
discouraged, for the Lord your God will be with you
wherever you go."
(Joshua 1:9, NIV)

CONTENTS

ABOUT THE AUTHOR AND ABOUT PT3D

Bert E. Wiseman is a bestselling author, teacher, and life coach. And he's been on a mission for the past 30 years. A mission to partner with parents to encourage reluctant readers to enjoy books.

Some books read like books, and some books read like movies. Bert writes books for children and teenagers that read like 3D movies; a natural storyteller well aware that the attention span of reluctant readers is even more so limited, Bert's writing style is the ever-present tension and action narrated in the present tense; he grabs you by the collar from the very first page and transcends you into the midst of action which is laid out like a storyboard of an action movie being created all around you. Reading a story written in past tense gives you the impression that the adventure is over and that the story is subsequently told to you; whereas when present tense is used, you experience the adventure as it's happening right now, all around you. It's the difference between watching a movie in 2D or 3D. The film storyline may be similar, but the experience is different. We call it PT3D, Present Tense 3D Reading Experience.

If you expect lengthy, artistic descriptions and complex character development, this may not be for you. If you're all about action and adventure, plot twists, wildly entertaining chases, where no speck of vulgarity creeps in, then you can shout 'Eureka!' — your teenage boys and girls are about to read a clean, thrilling book packed with adventure that both entertains and nurtures them alike. Bert's fans are typically in the range of 10-16 years of age, and his characters appeal to both Christian and secular audiences.

Bert E. Wiseman is an award-winning and established author of children and young people's books. He is popular in the Netherlands where he is known as Bert Wiersema; he has written over 60 bestsellers since starting his writing career in 1991, including several book series for younger children, teenagers and young adults, having sold half a million copies in a small country such as the Netherlands. Bert was part of the writing team for the 'Prentenbijbel' (published in English as 'The Beginning Reader's Bible'). He has also written 'Een regenboog in de woestijn' /'A Rainbow in the Desert' together with his daughter, Klarine Sikkema, a book about her battle with cancer while having a young family.

Please be a super trouper and leave a review on Amazon to let us know your thoughts about 'The Vaults of the Titanic' – this really helps us to reach more readers. Don't miss a beat - to learn more about Bert and to sign up for book news and giveaways, go to www.bertwisemanbooks.com. And if you're in the neck of the woods on social media, drop us a line on Facebook at www.facebook.com/BertWisemanBooks. We do like making new friends!

May the de Wolffs appeal to your imaginations as you meet them over the next pages,

Laura Wiersema

Editor

ABOUT THE DE WOLFF ADVENTURE SERIES

The de Wolff Adventure Series portrays an apparently ordinary family who could easily be your next door neighbours. Professor Willem de Wolff is a world renowned Dutch historian and academic often sought out for his expertise. He is married to Elise, and they have three teenage children — Bob, Eric, and Jessica. Together they travel the world as the professor gets invited to take part in expeditions, sometimes to retrieve artefacts of great value. These trips are not without danger as the valuables the professor is entrusted with tend to catch the attention of criminal networks. More often than not, what starts off as a working expedition for de Wolff and a holiday for the rest of the family, turns into a gripping and fast-paced adventure as they become embroiled in the schemes of unscrupulous people and must fight for survival.

Although occasionally the reading experience may be enhanced by reading previous installments, all of the books in the series make great standalone reads.

Bert's fans are typically in the range of 10-16 years of age, and often parents get hooked on the series themselves.

Chapter 1. A top secret mission

"MY NAME is Detective Lankhorst. I need to talk to you in private."

Professor Willem de Wolff is surprised to see the visitor on the doorstep of his home in Groningen. It's Friday night, and de Wolff is not expecting anybody. He picks up the expensive business card the detective hands out to him and sees that Mr Lankhorst really is on the payroll of a renowned detective agency with international contacts.

"Why do I have the pleasure of a visit from a private detective?" he asks a little suspiciously.

"If you have a moment, I'll explain," says the detective, with a friendly smile. "Sorry to arrive without warning; my clients are keen to keep things as quiet as possible."

The professor is unimpressed with this mysterious talk and decides to play for time before taking part in any secret discussions. "Come on in!" he says. "We can have a cup of coffee before we talk. My wife has just finished making some."

The detective allows himself to be led by the professor into the living room.

"This is Mr Lankhorst, a private detective," Willem de Wolff announces as he walks into the room. Elise de Wolff, the professor's wife, gets up from the chair where she's been reading. Jessica, Bob, and Eric — their three teenage children — immediately abandon their game of Risk at the table. The conquest of the world with a pair of coloured dice isn't nearly as interesting as a visit from a real live investigator!

"Wow!" Bob says enthusiastically. "Are you really a detective?"

"Eh, yes," replies Lankhorst, obviously embarrassed. De Wolff watches the reactions of his foreign guest closely. He's deliberately taken him into the room to get the measure of him.

"Do you have a gun with you?" Bob goes on.

"That's enough now, Bob!" intercedes his father while the detective regains his composure.

"Well, I have a gun license," he says. "I didn't think I'd need a gun. Was I mistaken?"

"Well, he's sometimes a little dangerous," jokes Bob, pointing with his thumb to his younger brother, Eric. Eric starts to respond, but the professor gestures them to silence and shows Mr Lankhorst to a chair.

Mrs de Wolff prepares some coffee while the kids try in vain to pick up the thread of their game. As Mr de Wolff talks with the detective, he asks some questions about the detective agency where Mr Lankhorst works.

"We're not exactly cheap," he says, "but you get what you pay for; we're the best in the business."

"You've made me curious," de Wolff admits.

Mrs de Wolff puts the coffee on the table and sits down on the couch.

"I know you wanted to talk privately," says the professor, "but hopefully you won't object to my wife being present. I don't have any secrets from her, and if you can't trust her, then you can't trust me. She'll be silent as the grave."

The kids realise they're about to be asked to leave. Bob in particular isn't happy; "things are just starting to get interesting", he thinks to himself.

"We can be silent as graves," he tries, but even this frank confession doesn't help.

"Go on upstairs, you three!" says their father. Reluctantly, they slide out of their seats and head out of the room.

"This sucks!" Bob growls once they're in the corridor. "What supersecrets could this guy have to talk about with mum and dad?"

"If they want you to know, they'll tell you," Jessica says with a flick of her hair, containing her own curiosity.

"You know what?" Bob whispers. "We could listen to them secretly behind the door."

"Don't be so childish!" Jessica rebukes him as she makes her way up the stairs.

"What do you think?" Bob pokes Eric.

"It must be something pretty important he's come here to talk about," replies Eric. "It's not often that we're sent away."

"Yeah, exactly!" Bob grumbles, but finding no support for his plans from the others, he unwillingly follows them upstairs.

"Please, begin your story!" prompts the professor.

The detective shifts in his chair. "I've got a proposal to make on behalf of my clients," he begins, "but before I do that, you must give me your word that everything I tell you will remain secret, even if you decide not to accept their offer."

"You have my word," promises the professor. Mrs de Wolff agrees too.

"I can only assume that you're knowledgeable about the Titanic," Lankhorst goes on.

"Certainly," replies the professor. "At the time the RMS Titanic was built, she was the largest and most luxurious passenger ship in the world. She was considered unsinkable, but on her first trip, in 1912 I think, she hit an iceberg and sank. It's still thought of as the deadliest maritime disaster in peacetime."

"You're familiar with the story," says Lankhorst. "Well, that's exactly what brings me here. I've been sent to you by the Sterling Ocean Company. Perhaps you've heard of them, but I'll fill you in. First, let's talk about where the Titanic fits in. You said yourself that it was a luxury ship. There were several millionaires on board when it sank. Many valuable treasures went to the bottom of the ocean. The water is over twelve thousand feet deep where the ship sank, and she was considered lost. At last, however, in 1985, the ship was discovered by the famous marine investigator, Robert Ballard. He took photos showing that the ship had broken down the middle; one half was found nine hundred yards away from the other. In 1994, a successful attempt was made to get a small unmanned submarine down to the wreck. The expedition was led by a French marine biologist who managed to retrieve various objects from the bottom; these were used to create an exhibition which travelled the world over; the display was a resounding success, and the costs of the expensive expedition were more than recouped. More expeditions were made at later dates, but the success of the first was never equalled. And now we come to where the Sterling Ocean Company fits in. The Company is led by the American billionaire, Hudson Sterling. He's currently setting up a new expedition and wants to re-enter the wreck to look for more artefacts. Sterling is a high flier who thinks big. He's recruited the same French diving team who were involved in the very first expedition. Now, he's looking for a number of renowned scholars to go with him on the trip to ensure that everything done is scientifically justified. Their job will be to record the retrieved objects and to decide the best thing to do with them. Our research suggests you would be an ideal candidate. You're known as a reliable scholar who is also an adventurer. The Sterling Ocean Company would like you to come on this Titanic Expedition as a scientific observer. You'll be there for quite some time, but I can assure you that it'll be worth your while. Money isn't a problem for Mr Sterling; he's in the top one hundred richest men in the world. He can arrange everything with your current employer. What do you think? "

The professor is elated. This is a childhood dream! A once in a lifetime opportunity! But he contains himself and merely asks:

"What makes Sterling think a new exhibition will be more successful than the first? Later exhibitions had considerably less interest. Will people who have seen the first exhibition be likely to go again?"

"We have reason to believe they will," replies the detective. "I'll show you something." He leans over and pulls his carefully locked briefcase towards him before he inserts a code and clicks it open. He takes out a bundle of photographs.

"These are photos taken when the mini submarine descended into the wreck. Look, you can even see the captain's bathtub!"

He selects a picture and pushes it towards the professor.

"What do you think this is?"

De Wolff and his wife consider the picture. There are a few bars and some metal objects, but they can't identify anything further.

"This photo was dismissed by the first expedition as unimportant. But the experts from the Sterling Ocean Company had access to all the pictures from the expedition and studied them again in more detail. They were particularly interested in this one. Do you recognize this object?"

De Wolff follows the detective's finger but still sees nothing special. Lankhorst delves into his briefcase again and grabs another picture from it. This picture shows a giant steel safe with a scroll wheel on the door. He points again to the first picture.

"My goodness," whispers de Wolff, "it's the corner of a safe!"

"Exactly!" chuckles the detective. "This photo was taken near the captain's cabin. Data verifies that the vaults were close to the captain's cabin, and this vault is accessible by submarine. It's likely there's a second safe close by. Presumably, you understand the significance. If the vaults were lifted, it would be world breaking news. They're likely to be packed with valuables. The first expedition just took everyday stuff: some fencing, some coal, even a jar of olives. The interest was overwhelming. The Titanic appeals to people's imaginations. What do you think would happen if the vaults were lifted? The interest would be greater than the treasures of Tutankhamun's tomb!"

"Probably so," de Wolff admits, "but then, why all the secrecy? Surely, the more attention the better. Turn to the press! Let it all be covered from day one in the papers!"

"No, definitely not!" Lankhorst asserts decidedly. "The previous expeditions drew a mixed response. More than fifteen hundred people drowned when the Titanic sunk. There were many people who thought they should be left to rest in peace."

"I can imagine," Mrs de Wolff says. "Not that long ago, the Estonia sank in the Baltic Sea, and over eight hundred people who couldn't abandon the ship in time drowned. The relatives would be furious if divers went down to the ship to try and salvage valuables."

"Precisely!" says Lankhorst. "But the difference is that the passengers who survived on the Titanic are no longer alive; it was that long ago. We believe enough time has passed to make it acceptable to dive to the wreck. But not everyone agrees with us, and we don't want a negative smear campaign in the press before the actual vaults are lifted. So until then, everything remains secret, and the press are kept out. "

"Suppose I should go," asks the professor, "when do I leave and when could I expect to be back?"

"The expedition leaves this summer. We're not sure when it will return, but it'll certainly take several months. Don't worry about your job at the university! The Sterling Company can arrange it all for you."

"It's not my job I'm primarily thinking of. We're rather a close-knit family, and I don't like the idea of being away for months at a time."

"Well," says Lankhorst, "these are decisions I can't help you with."

De Wolff thinks for a while; Mrs de Wolff doesn't interfere; she likes the fact that he's considering them, but she doesn't imagine he'll want to turn down such a unique venture. He'll never have an opportunity like it again.

"I'll make a counter proposal," the professor finally breaks the silence. "My job would be to clean and classify the extracted objects. I'm going to need some additional help with that. Let my wife and kids come along as my assistants. It won't cost Mr Sterling a penny extra."

Lankhorst thinks about it. "You'll understand I can't just say yes or no to that," he says. "My mission was to approach you, not to take on an additional four assistants."

"I understand," de Wolff nods, "but you tell Mr Sterling that if he wants me to come, I come with four assistants."

"Well," promises Lankhorst, "I'll tell him your terms. Meanwhile, you can look into the details. I have a flash drive with additional information that I can leave with you."

"Good," says de Wolff.

Lankhorst re-opens his briefcase and pulls out the flash drive. "This contains all the data: the logs from previous expeditions, all the pictures that were taken of the wreck, photos of the Titanic before she sank, the plans and so on. You'll be a Titanic expert by the time you've read all this information."

Professor de Wolff picks it up. "I'll start studying," he promises.

Lankhorst stands up and shakes hands with the professor and his wife. Then he picks up his briefcase from the floor. De Wolff and his wife accompany him to the door. The professor puts his arm around his wife, and together they watch Lankhorst walk to his car. The detective gets in, starts the engine, and pulls out into the traffic of Groningen.

"This could be the adventure of a lifetime!" exclaims the professor enthusiastically.

"Why?" a voice says behind his back. It's Bob who has flown down the stairs the moment he heard the detective leave.

De Wolff smiles at him broadly, his arm still round his wife. "We've promised to be as silent as two graves," he grins.

Later that evening, the professor sits down behind his computer. The kids have clearly been bursting with curiosity, and he's frustrated that he can't tell them anything; he's given his word to Lankhorst; he's honour bound. He's told them that he has been asked to consider joining a secret expedition, and that there's a chance they could go as a family. Meanwhile, they'll just have to be patient. They can manage that.

De Wolff puts the flash drive in and opens it up. He browses through various folders. The amount of information is mind blowing. He views a page with pictures of art works and pieces of jewellery that were thought to have been taken on the ship and presumably are still lying in the vaults. He whistles softly as he makes his way down the list and is suddenly struck with a nasty thought. Maybe Sterling has other reasons to stop the press becoming involved. Suppose the project comes to the attention of a criminal group? He doesn't like to think how a criminal organisation like the Mafia or Cosa Nostra might respond to the information that these famous vaults are going to be lifted. He puts the thoughts aside. It's ridiculous to think like that.

He continues browsing and comes across a document listing the names of everyone who has already pledged to go on the expedition to the icy sea grave of the Titanic. Each name has a short biography beside it. He notices that Sterling intends to join the trip himself. Further down, there's a list of various crew members, ranging from French divers to an American radio technician. He opens one at random and reads about the radio technician. It quickly becomes apparent that Sterling only hires the best of the best. Although the man has little more to do than operate the radio, he turns out to be renowned in the field of telecommunications. His name: Andy Howard. Living in Miami, Florida. Married. A five year old daughter.

Chapter 2. A nocturnal visit

Miami, Florida.

ANDY HOWARD is in bed. He's dreaming of the Titanic Expedition he was approached about a couple of weeks ago. Since he's been asked, he can think of little else. His wife initially had reservations about the fact that he'd be away from home for so long, but his excitement was so infectious that she found herself becoming increasingly happy for him. Now they are both sleeping soundly. They are oblivious to the dark car turning into their street.

The car pulls up under a canopy of trees. "Are you ready, Wesley?" asks the man behind the wheel.

Wesley nods. He opens the glove compartment and pulls out a couple of balaclavas. There are two strange looking guns and two pistols in there. They leave the pistols, and they each place one of the other weapons in their shoulder holsters. After taking a moment to check out the street and to be certain that they can't be seen, they step out of the car. Pulling on their balaclavas, they move quickly across the street, staying discreetly low. From there, they follow a narrow lane that takes them out behind the houses. There are no street lights here; the canopy of darkness continues to cover them. When they reach the Howard family's back gate, they stop. Wesley reaches for the handle, but Jack grabs his arm. He takes a little gadget from his pocket and presses a button. A small red light comes on. He starts scanning the fence with the device.

"What are you doing?" asks Wesley after Jack moves it carefully up one panel of fencing. He watches impatiently as his friend starts moving it painstakingly slowly down the next.

"Checking for an alarm," says Jack.

"Who has an alarm on their back gate?" queries Wesley.

"The guy who lives in this house is an electronic marvel. Do you think someone living in a luxury home with a talent for gadgetry isn't going to rig up some sort of intruder deterrent?" exclaims Jack. "This device reacts if it detects anything."

"And," Wesley sneers, "what are you expecting to find? A secret trapdoor? A machine gun hidden in the bushes? An ejector seat?"

Still sniggering, he grabs the handle of the gate. Instantly, he leaps back like he's been bitten by a snake. Putting his hand between his legs, he curses under his breath.

"According to my device," continues Jack steadily, "there's power running through the handle".

"Yes, I've identified that myself," says Wesley mournfully. "How do we get in there now?"

Jack pulls his balaclava off and wraps it round his hand. Very carefully he turns the handle, only to discover that the gate is locked. He takes a small torch from his pocket and lets the light glide over the lock. It's a simple lock that could be opened by a beginner if it didn't have an electric current running through it.

But Jack isn't a beginner. When it comes to electronics, he's every bit as good as Andy Howard, though perhaps, his talents have been employed for less scrupulous purposes.

"What are you doing?" whispers Wesley for a second time. He has now recovered and is looking with interest at his partner's actions. Jack pulls out his pocket knife and runs the blade between the fence and the post.

"That power didn't make its own way to the gate," Jack says calmly. "There's a cable hidden somewhere. Yes, there it is!"

The pocket knife has a plastic handle, allowing Jack to cut the wire without risking a shock. He checks the lock again and is satisfied to see the current has gone. Taking out a small tool set, he selects a tension wrench and quickly picks the lock. The gate swings open, and the two men make their way into the garden. Jack pulls his balaclava back over his face. They make their way up to the back door following the garden path. Wesley remains a respectful distance away while Jack uses the scanner again.

"Is there a current in that one as well?" hesitates Wesley.

Jack shakes his head. "But I didn't need a device to tell you that. You don't put a current through the door if you have a five year old child in the house. This door's fine, but it wouldn't surprise me if we found something else in the kitchen. Let's get through here first, anyway." He pulls the tool set out again and opens it silently. Holding up some picks to the light of the moon, he selects one; a little tinkering and the back door is open.

Jack turns around, "Stay here until I come and get you!" He turns the handle and pushes the door open inch by inch until it's just wide enough for him to slip through as stealthily as a cat. He stands for a moment, allowing his eyes to adjust to the darkness. He then pulls a pair of goggles from his pocket. Putting them on he sees the room again, but this time the image is computer generated, and he sees a number of lines crossing from wall to wall. It is just as he expected; Andy Howard's secured his home with laser beam sensors. If he breaks the beam, an alarm will go off. The goggles are able to detect and map the beams, so as long as he's wearing them, he can see where the beams are and avoid them. He turns around and sticks his head back out of the door.

"Don't, under any circumstances, come into the kitchen!" he warns Wesley. "The whole place is rigged with laser beams. You'll have to wait here until I get back."

He closes the door gently, leaving Wesley outside in the garden, and looks through the goggles again. Andy Howard is smart; the light beams are high enough for a five year old to easily pass under but low enough to be triggered by anyone taller — that is, anyone who doesn't know where they are. Jack sinks softly onto his hands and knees and crawls across the kitchen floor towards the hallway. The kitchen door is ajar, and he gently pushes it further open. Once in the doorway, he pauses. Still on his hands and knees, he gives his goggles time to map the hallway. Sure enough, it's rigged with laser beams too — one just behind the front door and one at the living room door. Jack takes out his torch, hopeful to see the control panel mounted in the hallway, but as he expected, it isn't, and the light beams continue across the stairs. There's nothing to be done but crawl up them. Deeply relieved that Wesley can't see how ridiculous he looks, he wriggles upstairs, and then lies down on his back on the landing between the upstairs rooms. Here at last, the goggles detect no more lights. He pulls them off. It's likely that the control panel is mounted around here somewhere. He lets his torch roam slowly over the walls and sees the panel to the left of the staircase. He gets quietly to his feet and examines it. It consists of a box about the size of a large book, and it's operated by a numerical code. A red light indicates that the alarm is active. Jack takes out a small screwdriver from his tool set. Carefully he loosens the two screws holding the cover in place. He stops after a few turns, knowing that the alarm will sound if the cover is fully lifted. Taking out a spring clip, he fastens the cover allowing him to finish removing the screws; then he uses the screwdriver to lift the cover just a fraction and slides the screwdriver in. He sources the pressure sensor and pushes the screwdriver against it to maintain the pressure, allowing him to remove the clip and let the cover fall to the ground. He searches again through his tool set, and he fishes out a small pair of nail scissors. Holding the little torch in his mouth to illuminate his work, he lifts up a few of the visible cables, and using the nail scissors, he cuts through them. As the last cable is cut, the red light goes out. The alarm is deactivated. Jack slowly eases the pressure on the sensor and then removes the screwdriver entirely. No sound! He walks lightly down the stairs, and no alarms greet him. He goes to the back door, opens it, and motions Wesley inside.

"I was starting to think you wouldn't be back," Wesley growls. Deep down, Wesley's a bit jealous of Jack's expertise. Wesley's role revolves more around brawn than brain. But then, both are essential to the criminal organisation they belong to. Jack pulls his weapon from his holster and goes back into the kitchen. Wesley takes his in his hand and follows his partner.

Back upstairs, Jack opens one of the doors. Behind it is the bathroom. Not what they're looking for. The second door opens to reveal a large bedroom. Against the wall is a double bed, and under the blankets two bumps indicate that the bed is occupied. With silent steps the two men approach the bed. Andy Howard is gently snoring. Next to him sleeps his wife; she's pretty; her long blonde hair lies like a halo round her sleeping head. Jack and Wesley stand either side of the bed, point their weapons at the sleeping couple, and pull the triggers. There are two soft popping sounds. Andy bounces up for a moment, his face contorted with pain, and then slumps back on his pillow. His wife doesn't make a sound.

"Those tranquilliser guns work perfectly," chuckles Wesley. "That guy was out for the count the minute it hit."

Jack nods. "Let's get on with it then." They pull back the covers roughly, and Wesley grabs Ruth Howard under her arms while Jack picks up her ankles. They carry her down the stairs, through the front door, and into the garden. Now, outside they have to be more careful. Keeping low again, they walk down the lane checking the street before moving across the road and placing her quickly in the back of the car. Wesley slides in behind the wheel and drives away. Jack swaps his tranquilliser gun for his pistol and walks leisurely back to the Howards' house. Once inside, he closes the door behind him and walks up the stairs to the bedroom. Pulling round a chair, he sits down next to the bed and puts the bedside lamp on. He expects Andy to start to come round in about an hour. Jack leans back in his chair and settles down to wait patiently.

Andy half opens his eyes. He feels dizzy. His mouth is dry, and there's a foul taste in it. Groaning, he pulls himself upright, opens his eyes fully, and blinks in surprise at the light of the bedside lamp. He's usually awake earlier than Ruth. He turns, curious to see if she's lying beside him, and with a cry, falls back into his pillows. She's not there. Instead, there's a man sitting beside the bed — with a balaclava over his face — and there's a gun pointing at him.

"Who are you? How did you get in? Where's my wife?!!"

"That's three questions," Jack says quietly. "I'm not going to answer the first two, but I'll help you with the third. Your wife is safe, but if you want it to stay that way, you're going to need to listen to me."

"What do you want?" utters Andy, now rather scared. "We don't have a lot of money."

"We know your bank balance," Jack continues. "We're not looking for money. Two weeks ago, you signed up for an expedition to the Titanic with the Sterling Ocean Company."

"How do you know that?" Andy sounds startled. "That's top secret."

Jack chuckles softly behind his balaclava.

"There are not many secrets kept from our organisation. But let's get to the point. You're going to be operating the radio. We want you to keep us informed of any developments on board. We want to know every object that's lifted from the seabed, especially if it concerns the vaults. We also want to know exactly when the expedition leaves. "

"Why do you want to know? What are you planning?" Andy demands an answer.

"That's not something you need to know," replies Jack.

"But it would be a betrayal of the Sterling Ocean Company."

"I suppose your family is important to you?"

"Yes, of course, but ....."

"No buts," Jack says sharply. "I'm leaving now. You'll be reunited with your wife shortly. We'll be in touch. Oh, and one more thing . . . don't tell the police anything."

Jack gets up, refusing to listen to any more questions. He runs down the stairs, out the door, and pulling the door shut behind him, he is gone.

Andy's left in turmoil. Instinctively, he grabs the phone from his bedside table to dial the police, but then he rapidly puts it down again. No police! But what should he do? Still weak at the knees, he stumbles out of bed. The first thing he sees on the landing is the open control panel, but he can worry about that later. Passing it by, he runs to his daughter's bedroom, and with a pounding heart, looks into the little bed. She's sleeping peacefully on her back having missed the entire nocturnal adventure. Relieved, Andy leaves the room and returns to the landing. He examines the damaged control panel. It doesn't take long to see that the break in was no amateur job. Silently, he goes down the stairs and checks every room, but if he's expecting to find Ruth, he'll be bitterly disappointed.

Ruth Howard is on a bench in a Miami park, in her nightgown, barely a mile away from her own home. Wesley took her there as previously agreed with Jack. Shivering, Ruth opens her eyes. She feels cold and miserable. She suddenly realises she's on a hard wooden plank. With a squeal, she gets up and looks around in surprise. The early morning light shines on the trees. She recognises the park she often walks in with little Karen. How did she end up here? Could she have been sleepwalking? But that has never happened to her before, and if so, how would she have made it past the alarm system? She sees someone scavenging in a bin on the other side of the pond, and she gets up quickly. She doesn't want to stay here a moment longer. The gravel hurts her feet, and she moves off the path onto the grass and leaves the park through a large gate. A young newspaper boy has already started his work. She stumbles up onto the pavement, feeling alone and vulnerable in her nightgown. She jumps as a car stops next to her, and she looks inside. To her relief, she realises it's a police car. The policeman gets out.

"Are you ok?" he asks, looking concerned. "What are you doing out here?"

"I don't know," Ruth says suddenly sniffing, unable to hold back her tears any longer. Her confusion and the embarrassment at being out on the street in her nightgown are suddenly too much. "I woke up in the park. I don't know how I got here."

"Where do you live then?" asks the policeman.

"A few blocks away," she says. "I think I must have been sleepwalking."

"Has anything like this ever happened to you before?"

"No, never. Not that I'm aware of anyway."

The policeman puts his arm around her and guides her to the police car. "We'll take you home," he says reassuringly.

Chapter 3. Hanging by a thread

ANDY DOESN'T LOOK very surprised when a police car turns into his drive. He's sitting in the living room deciding how to react to the visit when he sees Ruth getting out of the car. He jumps up, flings the front door open, and joyfully throws his arms around her.

"What have they done to you?" he exclaims. "Where did they take you?"

"They?" Ruth asks. "What are you talking about?"

"The guys who kidnapped you," he whispers in the hope that the policeman who stepped out of the car behind her can't hear.

"Kidnapped?" Ruth asks, a little too loudly. "I think I've been sleepwalking."

The policeman overhears. Becoming suspicious, he goes over to Andy and introduces himself.

"You thought your wife had been kidnapped?" he asks.

"Uh, yeah, so to speak," stammers Andy.

"If I can't find my wife in the morning, that's not the first conclusion I draw," replies the officer. Andy's unsure what to say, and then he decides to be frank.

"Please come in, we're in trouble!" he says softly.

Once inside, he directs the officer to a chair and then, sitting down himself, he starts to talk about the hooded man who was in his bedroom in the morning.

"What did he want from you?" the policeman asks. Andy doesn't dare tell him the whole truth.

"I've been asked to work on a secret project and these guys want me to abandon it," he says. It made little sense to let Ruth know that they asked him to work for them.

"What secret project?" the policeman enquires further.

"Unfortunately I can't tell you about it," says Andy. "I promised confidentiality." Then he jumps to his feet. "I need police protection!" he says anxiously. "Those guys will be back. I have a good alarm system in my house, but they just walked straight in. Now that I've taken you into my confidence, they'll be back for me."

The policeman makes a reassuring gesture. "I'll contact the office immediately. If you need protection, I won't leave here until it's in place."

Andy looks at the policeman gratefully and feels a wave of relief. It seems he's made the right decision taking him into his confidence.

Little Karen Howard sits on her chair in her classroom. She listens to the exciting story the primary school teacher's telling. Outside, in the car park, is an inconspicuous car containing a plain clothed policeman. He's to pick up little Karen when she finishes school in about half an hour. The Howard family have indeed been offered protection. All three family members have been allocated an officer to keep them under surveillance. Bored with reading his sports magazine, the policeman glances up as a van parks next to him. Two men in overalls step out and walk to the rear of the truck. Losing interest, the officer glances at his watch and then turns back to his magazine.

Suddenly, the door next to him is pulled open, and before he can react, a needle is pushed through his clothes and into his arm. He tries to defend himself, but everything starts to spin around him. One more blow from his attacker, and he crumples forward over the wheel. Strong hands pull him out, grab his identification and police badge from him, and drag him to the van. He's thrown in the back and the doors slam shut.

One man climbs in behind the wheel of the van. The other pulls off his overalls to reveal a smart suit not unlike the one the policeman was wearing. He puts the identity card and police badge in his pocket and gives the driver a nod. The engine starts, and the van drives off. The other man gets into the policeman's car. He looks at his watch. The whole operation lasted only a few seconds. Just a short time to wait, and he can go pick up little Karen.

Andy's startled when he opens the door and sees the face of Inspector Hutchinson.

"I have a message for you," says the Inspector hesitantly.

"Karen! She was due home ages ago." Andy's voice rises to a shout. "What's happened to her?"

"Unfortunately, we don't know," admits the Inspector. "She was picked up from school this afternoon but not by one of our men. The officer who was due to collect her has vanished."

The afternoon has become a nightmare for Andy and Ruth. More policemen arrive after the Inspector. One by one, they do their best to reassure the Howard couple, but the bustling officers just make the worried parents even more anxious. Andy wishes he never involved the police. They were apparently no match for the intruders. What will those guys do with his daughter? He can't bear thinking that he might lose her. Initially, the Howards thought they couldn't have children; the doctors were amazed when Ruth became pregnant. He'd give literally anything to see Karen again. Sighing, he watches one of the experts from the police force attempt to set up his phone so that any call from the kidnappers will be automatically recorded. But his thoughts are with Karen. She's a highly intelligent girl and wise beyond her years. He enjoys the talks they have together. He feels tears burning behind his eyes.

More than an hour passes. To the Howards relief, a number of the officers leave, and only the Inspector and his assistant lag behind. They sit silently in the living room watching the phone. Ruth heads to the kitchen to make some coffee and something to eat, not that anyone said they were hungry, but she needs to do something; sitting in the room with those three silent men is making her nervous, and she can barely resist the urge to scream. Suddenly, she stiffens. The bell has just rung.

Andy leaps up from his chair. Could that be one of the kidnappers? They would hardly dare to come here in broad daylight and ring the doorbell. They must know the police are here. Not knowing what to do, he looks at the Inspector.

"Go see who's there!" whispers the Inspector. "Unless it's something to do with Karen, get rid of them. Curious neighbours are the last thing we need."

Andy nods and goes off down the corridor. He sees Ruth at the kitchen door. She looks taut as a wire as she's standing with one hand to her mouth. He walks slowly to the front door; if only they had one with a glass panel! With a pounding heart, he looks through the small peep hole. To his surprise he can't see anyone. Maybe he's taken too long getting there. A soft knock on the door follows. Andy shrinks back a bit, but then gathering his courage, he pulls the door open. His mouth drops open in shock and amazement.

"Karen!" he yells.

There on the doorstep stands his daughter! She looks surprised at her father's reaction, who swiftly finds himself pushed aside by his wife. Ruth lifts her daughter from the doorstep, and squeezes her like she'll never let go. The Inspector and his assistant appear behind her.

Ruth carries Karen into the living room where she's besieged with questions. At first, she's a bit overwhelmed, but then she begins to chat about where she's been.

"There was a policeman at school," she says. "He picked me up. We've been a bit naughty. He said we were meant to go home, but instead we went to an ice cream shop and had an ice cream to eat. It was yummy. I got banana ice cream with whipped cream. After that, we went to the playpark, and then we came home. "

"Where's the policeman who brought you here?" asks Hutchinson.

"He didn't have time to come in, he said he had to go home to eat," replies the girl.

Hutchinson begins to understand.

"What did this policeman look like?" he asks.

"He was very tall and had funny red hair," laughs the girl.

"The policeman who was guarding her was a squat powerhouse with almost white hair," he says to his assistant. "It must have been one of the kidnappers. But why have they brought her back?" he adds thoughtfully, and then looks at the girl intently. "Did the policeman say anything to you about your father? Did he say there was something he wasn't allowed to do?"

The girl shakes her head resolutely.

"Did he give you anything?"

Again the girl shakes her head and then smiles mysteriously.

"Why are you laughing?" asks the Inspector, a little irritated.

"It's nothing," replies the girl, still with a smile on her lips.

Hutchinson isn't sure what to do.

"I suspect the kidnappers will be in touch during the course of the evening," he tells Andy. "You know the call will be recorded automatically. Please contact me if you hear from them." He gets up from his chair. "We'll leave you in peace for now. We have two officers who will monitor the front and back of your house. One is sitting in a car across the road just like last night. Have a torch ready! If the kidnappers call, flash the light through the window, and the officer will come over straight away."

Andy nods, happy that the police are leaving. What will the criminals ask of him? He's willing to bet they want the police out of the picture. But Hutchinson doesn't seem to him like the sort of man who will be easily dismissed. With mixed feelings, Andy sees the Inspector out.

When he comes back into the room, he sees, to his surprise, that his daughter is sitting beaming at him.

"It worked!" she almost cheers.

"What worked?" asks Ruth, startled.

"The game," laughs the girl.

"What game?" Andy says slowly. He feels a sudden knot in his stomach.

"The game the policeman and I made up. He was so nice. He said the officers would be annoyed that I was late home, and they'd be a little upset. We agreed I wouldn't tell them anything. And I didn't! "

"What were you not to tell?" Andy asks.

Karen leans forward in excitement.

"I have a secret note for you," she whispers, her eyes sparkling. "A note for Dad. But I was only to give it to you when the silly policemen had gone."

"Quickly, give it to me!" Andy says with an intensity that scares Karen. Taken aback, she pulls a crumpled piece of paper from her pocket. Andy grabs it from her. A letter from the kidnappers. They fooled his daughter. She thinks this is all some funny game, but nothing could be further from the truth. With trembling fingers, he unfolds the paper.

Dear Mr Howard,

Apparently, abducting your wife wasn't enough to convince you that we mean business, which is why we've given you another small demonstration of what we're capable of. We trust you're now convinced that we're a force to be reckoned with and are willing to do what we ask.

Proceed as follows: tell the police you no longer require their protection; then at midnight, call the phone number at the bottom of this letter; you will then receive further instructions from us. If you don't call at midnight, or you liaise with the police again, we will consider you uncooperative, and we'll take whatever measures we feel necessary. The Sterling Ocean Company will then require another radio technician who will undoubtedly be more willing to cooperate with us after he hears what's happened to you.

P.S. Please understand that killing someone is much easier than abducting them.

There's a phone number at the bottom. Ashen-faced, Andy hands the letter to Ruth. She reads it with growing horror.

"What are you going to do?" she whispers.

"I'll work with them," said Andy. "The alternative is a bullet in my body from a long-range rifle."

"But you can't call!" whispers Ruth. "Every call is recorded automatically."

"It'll be easy enough for me to dismantle the recording equipment," Andy replies. "If only I didn't involve the police! It seemed like the perfect solution, but it's turning into a nightmare."

Later that evening, Andy sabotages the recording equipment, and with pursed lips calls the number.

Chapter 4. The adventure begins

"TOO BAD," sighs Bob. "This could have been amazing."

He looks glumly out of the round window of the small jet plane that's taxiing down the runway at Groningen Airport. It could have been a beautiful view, but it's completely hidden by fog.

"When you're in luxury seating, you don't need a view for a good flight experience," says his father stroking the lining of the chair. "I wouldn't mind having a chair like this at home. It makes me feel a bit like a king."

"I feel more like a sausage roll," chuckles Jessica who's put her seat back and is lying snuggled into her pillows, her long blond wavy hair fanned out around her. She looks sleepily across at her mother who has also nestled into her chair.

Eric, like his brother, concentrates on trying to catch sight of something through the misty wreaths.

The five of them are on their way to their first meeting with Mr Sterling and the rest of the team. Professor de Wolff accepted the position on the basis that he could bring the rest of the family as scientific assistants. There followed a couple of tense weeks while they waited for final confirmation, until eventually, Detective Lankhorst came to let them know the whole family had been given permission to come. Eric in particular was overjoyed. What could be more thrilling then an expedition to the Titanic?!

He wanted to shout about it from the mountaintops, but unfortunately, he wasn't even allowed to tell his closest friends. Bob is excited too, but mostly because they'll be away considerably longer than the school holidays would normally last. He's also excited about the experience of being on the ship along with the divers and adventurers. Jessica likes the fact that for a few weeks it will just be the family all together.

They've all got their reasons to look forward to the adventure, and it's already off to a good start. Mr Sterling is one of the richest people in the world, and it's evident that he's used to having the best. They're now flying in a private jet to Rotterdam where there will be a taxi waiting to pick them up and bring them to Scheveningen. Mr Sterling will meet them at the Kurhaus Hotel which is where they'll spend the night.

Mrs de Wolff puts her hand on her husband's arm. "Isn't it crazy to think that we'll be sleeping in one of the most luxurious hotels in the country tonight?"

"Yes," laughs the professor. "If I were you, I'd stay awake all night — shame to waste those precious hours sleeping."

The plane takes off and quickly rises into the clouds. Now there's literally nothing to be seen outside.

Eric pulls his bag towards him so he can retrieve the book his father bought him. It's about the Titanic; he's read it so often that he nearly knows it by heart. On the cover is a picture of the doomed ship slowly sinking into the waves. It must have been an incredible sight. On 10 April 1912, she left the port of Southampton on her maiden voyage as the largest and most luxurious ship in the world. Many millionaires signed up to take part in the historic journey. What a historic trip it turned out to be, though not for the reasons they had expected! After all, they thought the Titanic was unsinkable. The bulkheads meant to ensure that, even if the ship was holed, it would stay afloat. The shipbuilder was very proud of it and stated in an interview, 'even God himself can't sink this ship.' There are times when humanity believes it can do better than God. In that sense, the Titanic was like a floating tower of Babel: an impressive example of human accomplishment. But God is not impressed at such pride.

The captain was also thought to be a safe pair of hands. Captain Edward Smith was one of the most experienced sailors in the world. No, there was really nothing that could go wrong. And yet the worst happened. Despite the warning reports of icebergs in the area, the Titanic continued to sail at high speed. The captain was afterwards blamed for his recklessness and held responsible for the tragedy. However, later evidence gave rise to the theory that there might have been an uncontrollable fire in one of the coal bunkers on board, and the crew had been directed to get to New York as quickly as possible to get it under control. Why the Titanic sailed at such speed through dense fog in the North Atlantic will probably never be known. But when it was reported that there was an iceberg straight ahead, there was no possibility of avoiding it. Had the Titanic collided head on, it might only have sustained damage to the bow, and left the passengers shaken but unharmed. However, the ship turned to try and avoid the collision, and the sharp ice cut along the side slicing it open like a sardine tin. The bulkheads flooded; they could no longer keep the ship afloat, and the proud Titanic was doomed to sink. It was only some time later that the passengers realised the extent of the disaster. There weren't enough lifeboats to rescue everybody; women and children were the first to leave the ship, with the wealthy in first class being prioritized, whilst others were left behind. Barriers keeping the second and third class passengers in were only opened at the last minute, and by then, it was too late for most of them to escape. There was little point in jumping into the sea as it would only be possible to survive a few minutes in the icy water. The radio operator continued to broadcast distress signals until the last possible moment. Every ship in the area rushed to help. The nearest ship was over an hour away, but before she could reach the site of the disaster, the Titanic disappeared under the waves dragging more than fifteen hundred people with her.

The disaster was world news, and the tragic story of the ship still has global appeal. To this day, there are new books, documentaries, and even feature films about the disaster. The book Eric is holding in his hands has only just been published.

With a sigh he flips it shut. In the weeks to come, he'll be at that very spot, the wreck resting on the seabed about twelve thousand feet below him. A small double submarine equipped with cameras will dive down, and everyone on board will be able to watch on large screens as it descends to the ship. Few people in the world will ever experience something like that.

"Hey, it's clearing up!" Bob says enthusiastically. He points out of the window, and Eric puts his book down and looks outside. Sure enough, the clouds are breaking, and it's possible to look down and see everything below. The others move over to the windows to take the scenery in, and then all too soon, they find themselves descending into Rotterdam Airport. Gathering their hand luggage, they head into the airport.

A taxi driver jumps up from a chair in the Arrivals Hall and walks towards the de Wolffs.

"Professor de Wolff and his scientific assistants?" he asks a little hesitantly as he takes in the children.

"That's us," Bob grins broadly.

"OK," replies the driver making no further comment. "Your taxi awaits."

Five minutes later, their bags are in the boot, and they're on their way to Scheveningen.

The first sight of the Kurhaus is a little disappointing. Not that it isn't pretty, quite the contrary. The stately hotel still has a beautiful appearance, but it's hemmed in by modern concrete buildings and looks a bit out of place in between them; a bit like a Rembrandt in a modern art museum.

The taxi drops them off outside.

"Wow," says Eric approvingly as they look up at the facade. "Doesn't look bad to me!"

"Do you think we're dressed smartly enough?" Jessica whispers to her mum.

Her mother shrugs. "They can take us as we are," she says. De Wolff goes to get the suitcases out of the car, but two hotel clerks hastily appear and claim the bags before he can get to them. The little procession moves inside. It's immediately evident that they're in the top hotel in the country. The hall is magnificent. Left and right are small expensive shops, and a grand marble staircase leads up to a beautiful restaurant. They head up the stairs and emerge in the restaurant feeling a bit overwhelmed. A man gets up from where he's been sitting. He's dressed in a neat white suit and wears a white cowboy hat.

"I'm guessing that's Mr Sterling," says the professor as the tall figure moves towards them. The man has long grey hair emerging from under his hat, and a moustache graces his upper lip.

"He looks a bit like Buffalo Bill," says Eric who's seen a picture of the famous gunfighter.

The American greets them with an outstretched hand. "Willem de Wolff and family?" he asks.

"Yes," replies the professor shaking the offered hand.

Hudson Sterling leads them to a table at the back where he introduces them to his wife, Goldie Sterling, and the expedition's doctor, Dr Reynolds. Elise de Wolff is pleased to see that there will be another woman on board. Goldie is outgoing and friendly, and the two women are soon chatting away comfortably. Mr Sterling makes sure everyone has coffee and sips away on an espresso himself while the group get to know one another. They are told the French diving team is also staying at the hotel. The team is out in the city at the moment, but they will join them for dinner tonight. They'll meet the crew on the ship in Rotterdam tomorrow. For now, they're invited to go to their rooms to freshen up.

"Do you play chess?" Sterling asks as de Wolff is about to leave.

"A little," the professor says modestly.

"Then we should definitely play sometime," laughs the billionaire. "I'm almost addicted to chess."

"That's fine by me," agrees de Wolff.

A valet takes them to their hotel rooms. The professor and his wife have a suite with a sea view. The children each have a separate room with bath, toilet, and all the extras you would expect from a hotel like the Kurhaus. Bob takes a huge dive onto his bed.

The professor and his wife stand on the balcony and watch the busy boulevard beneath them. "Well, Elise," he smiles, "are you enjoying this taster of how the rich live?"

"I'm not sure I really fit in," she says. "Looking around the room makes me realise just how ordinary I am."

"Not to me!" smiles the professor, putting his arm around her.

At the same time as the professor's talking with his wife in the Kurhaus, an enormous Cadillac is drawing up alongside the equally luxurious Metropolitan Hotel in New York. The car windows are darkened making it impossible to see inside. The driver opens the rear door, and a burly man with mirrored sunglasses steps out. The man is in his fifties, with short dark hair and a determined looking chin. He stands proud like an army colonel. Few people know that he's called Mortimer. Edward Mortimer. Even fewer people know that he's the leader of one of the most dangerous criminal organisations in the world. He strides confidently into the hotel lounge and spots the man he's looking for, one of his subordinates.

"What's the latest on the Titanic expedition?" he asks after he's checked they're out of earshot.

"Everything's going to schedule," replies the man. "The ship's now in the port at Rotterdam ready to take the Dutch professor on board. They'll leave for Iceland tomorrow afternoon where the last expedition member is being picked up, and then they'll set sail for the wreck."

"And the radio technician is with us?" Mortimer asks.

The other man smiles. "He's as docile as a sheep," he says. "He contacts us every day with updates."

"Excellent!" Mortimer exclaims in measured tones. "I'm expecting the others here in the course of the evening, and then I'll go over my plans."

Chapter 5. Diamonds are forever

"I DON'T LIKE that René du Nord," Bob grumbles. "I don't know why the conceited gorilla thinks so much of himself."

"Don't let him hear you say that!" Eric laughs. "He'll hit your head so hard you'll be looking out from between your ribs."

"I think I'm okay," chuckles Bob. "He doesn't understand Dutch."

They're walking along the Scheveningen pier as they discuss the leader of the French diving team. They met the French team over dinner last night. The team seemed friendly enough despite the kids not understanding a word of French. Only the leader of the squad was unpleasant, a man with a neck like a hippopotamus and muscles like cannonballs. Firstly, he gave them handshakes that made their bones crack, and from then on he ignored them completely. Later, they heard that René du

Nord had strongly opposed the decision to allow children on board, and Mr Sterling had had trouble persuading him not to drop out of the expedition altogether. Last night, Mr Sterling took the children aside and discreetly asked them to keep their distance from the divers, to which they immediately agreed. Actually, they privately agreed that it was unusual for kids to be on an expedition like this, but it didn't seem to bother Mr Sterling. He told them that he had two boys their age. Eric liked the idea of having two American boys to run about with on the ship; it soon became clear that they wouldn't join the expedition as Mr Sterling explained that the boys were away at a summer camp.

"At least Sterling is a good guy," says Bob.

"And he's the boss," laughs Eric. "I think it's more important that we get on well with him than with the French Bulldozer."

"Didn't you want to go with mum and Jess?" asks Bob, changing the subject.

"Are you crazy?" Eric said. "Looking in all the clothes shops with a bunch of women? No way!"

"Oh, I don't know," Bob says, thoughtfully. "Shopping with a billionaire must have its upsides."

Elise de Wolff and Jessica have reached the same conclusion. They're walking through the centre of The Hague with Goldie Sterling, enjoying shopping with someone who doesn't need to count the pennies. Despite this, they are starting to feel increasingly uncomfortable.

The idea of going shopping was sparked last night when the divers, the scientific team, and the crew agreed to a meeting the following day at the hotel to discuss the details of the expedition. Mrs Sterling suggested a shopping spree in The Hague instead. Bob and Eric weren't interested, but Mrs de Wolff and Jessica were keen to go.

The girls get along just fine. Mrs de Wolff's English holds up well, and Jessica — the oldest of the three kids — knows enough to follow the conversation, though the charmingly eccentric Mrs Sterling does a lot of the talking anyway. They have a quick look inside the Dutch parliament, but Mrs Sterling is easily bored. She wants to go into the renowned Meddens across the road. Mrs de Wolff and Jessica nearly fall over in astonishment when Mrs Sterling nonchalantly purchases a huge Persian carpet on sale at almost thirty thousand euros.

"You won't be able to take that on board," Mrs de Wolff points out.

"That's quite alright, it will simply be delivered to my home in America. Additional costs? Not a problem," responds Mrs Sterling matter-of-factly.

And so it goes on with a range of expensive perfumes being purchased next. Mrs de Wolff and Jessica glance at each other. Shopping is fun, but this is becoming excessive. It becomes even more uncomfortable when Mrs Sterling starts buying gifts for them. After a short hesitation, Mrs de Wolff accepts a fragrant Chanel perfume, and Jessica is given a pretty silk scarf. They make it clear that they don't want anything else, although they don't turn down the coffee and cake Mrs Sterling buys for them.

"She parts with her money awfully easily," Jessica whispers to her mother when Mrs Sterling is at the toilet.

"Yes," her mother says, "if you have the money you might treat yourself a little more, but I'm not sure about spending as wildly as she does, especially when you think of all the suffering in the world."

"Do you think we should say something?" Jessica asks uncertainly.

Mrs de Wolff thinks for a moment. She doesn't want to say anything to damage their friendship, but on the other hand, she doesn't like talking behind people's backs.

"Maybe if the opportunity comes up," she says.

The opportunity presents itself sooner than they expect. In an upmarket clothes shop, Mrs Sterling sees a dress she thinks would look great on Mrs de Wolff.

"That dress costs more than my wedding dress!" replies Mrs de Wolff. "I wouldn't want to spend so much on a dress."

"But you don't have to pay for it," Mrs Sterling assures her enthusiastically.

"I've already got a lovely gift from you," Mrs de Wolff says. "I'm quite happy with that."

Mrs Sterling shakes her head. "My husband makes a lot of money," she goes on. "It would be nothing for us. Peanuts."

"In Africa that amount of money could feed an orphanage for a month," Mrs de Wolff says before she has time to think about it. She waits a little anxiously for the reaction of the billionaire.

But Mrs Sterling is unembarrassed. "I'll try to hold back a bit," she adds with a wink.

Thankfully, as promised, the wealthy American reins in her spending, and later she even agrees to take a look at the Prison Gate Museum — a medieval prison complete with torture devices. She emerges disgusted, and at her suggestion, they head to the Omniversum to watch a 3D film about space. Mrs de Wolff and Jessica come out feeling a bit dizzy, but all things considered, the three of them have had a wonderful morning together.

The taxi brings them back to the Kurhaus, and they're just about to walk in when Mrs Sterling glances to the right and notices a small but prestigious jewellery shop.

"Let's have a look!" she says taking her two companions with her.

Once inside, the door shuts fast. The jeweller will press a button to release it when they are ready to go, making it impossible for anyone to grab an item and run. But the three women are not there to steal. Jessica feels like she's in the treasure rooms of Tutankhamun. It's such a dazzling shop. Her eye falls on a beautiful ring with a diamond about half a centimetre in diameter set in it. It sparkles brilliantly as the light catches it, and whenever she moves, she sees the light at a different angle. Mrs Sterling notices the girl.

"Take it!" she prods Jessica gently. "Try it!"

Jessica's shocked and immediately embarrassed to have been caught looking, but Mrs Sterling orders the ring to be taken out of the display cabinet. It slides onto Jessica's finger as if it were made for her. The saleswoman is enthusiastic in her praise and offers Jessica a mirror. Jessica, still uncomfortable, just nods a bit. She has long slender fingers which complement the ring, and it really does look fantastic on her. Mrs de Wolff looks a bit worried. Surely Mrs Sterling isn't planning on buying the ring! But it looks like she is. As the American pulls her purse out, Mrs de Wolff grabs her arm.

"This is crazy!" she says firmly. "I'm going to have to say no. You've been kind enough. We don't need anything else from you."

"Oh, I don't feel I have to," Mrs Sterling assures her. "I'm just enjoying this outing with your daughter, and it's a pleasure to see her happy. I've always wanted a daughter, but I've only got boys in the house, and this kind of thing doesn't appeal to them at all. If it isn't fast and noisy, they're not interested."

The saleswoman understands what's going on and picks up the platinum card from the counter.

"Shall I package it for you?" she asks. But Mrs Sterling shakes her head.

"Jewellery should be worn," she decides.

Mrs de Wolff lets things take their course. She feels wrong-footed by the wealthy American, but not wanting a confrontation, she doesn't force Jessica to give the jewellery back. Moments later, Jessica is walking down the marble stairs as if in a dream. With the diamond sparkling on her finger, she feels as if everyone's looking at her. Mrs Sterling puts her arm around her.

"Think of it as a memorial to the Titanic expedition. Diamonds are beautiful. 'Diamonds are forever', we say in America."

"If I had only known!" Bob says, angry at himself.

"Then what?" asks the professor.

"Then I'd have gone shopping, of course," replies Bob.

The five of them are in Mr and Mrs de Wolff's suite, and Jessica has just shyly shown them the ring.

"What did it cost?" asks Eric sounding interested but feeling a bit jealous.

Mrs de Wolff tells them.

"Wow!" sighs Bob. "What could I have bought for that amount of money?!"

"A lot!" admits his mother. "But we felt quite embarrassed today."

"That's something I wouldn't have had a problem with," says Bob. "Why not let the rich folk treat you? They still have plenty of money."

"I don't agree with that approach," his mother says. "That woman has spent tens of thousands of Euros today on things that are totally unnecessary. I'm not comfortable with that."

"Why not?" Bob says, a bit cheekily.

"I'm not sure that sits well with our lifestyle," his mother says. "I prefer a more modest life".

"What do you mean?" Eric wants to know.

Mrs de Wolff searches for the right words.

"You need to control yourself a little," says Mr de Wolff. "Of course it's fine to enjoy some luxuries. We've got things at home we don't need, and we bought them because we happened to like them. But there needs to be a limit."

Bob is quick to disagree. "It depends how you look at it," he says. "If you've got the option to spend a million every day, and you only spend one hundred thousand, then you've been pretty modest. Just think about it."

The professor shakes his head, smiling at the immovable teenage logic.

"What does it matter?" says Eric. "We don't have a million to spend every day."

"Even one day would be pretty good fun," chuckles Bob.

"Come on," says Jessica, "money can't buy you happiness."

"Maybe," Bob retorts, "but having no money doesn't make you happy either."

"Shall we talk about something other than money?" Mrs de Wolff cuts in, a little annoyed.

"OK," says Bob. "But next time you go shopping, I'm coming!"

Jessica takes another look at her ring and asks, "What do they mean in America when they say 'diamonds are forever'?"

"It means diamonds stay perfect," says Mr de Wolff. "They don't wear out. Diamonds are the hardest material in the world. For example, you can use it to cut glass without the diamond being damaged."

"I'm going to put it in a safe place," promises Jessica. "That way it will definitely stay beautiful."

"Not at all!" says her father. "It's a pity to have such a beautiful piece of jewellery only to put it in a drawer. Now that you have it, wear it! It looks good on you."

In a spacious room at the Metropolitan Hotel in New York, a group of men sit round a large table. At the head is Mortimer. "Gentlemen," he begins, "the Titanic Expedition is about to leave. In about a week, they will arrive at the location where the wreck lies thousands of feet below. They will try to pick up as many objects as possible, just like the expedition that visited the wreck in 1994. These items will be of great value even if they're sold on the black market; it's important we get them into our possession. We also need the files and the films that prove they're authentic. But there's more —" He waits for a moment allowing the tension to build.

" — what nobody knows is that they will also look for the vaults of the Titanic. Two vaults that nobody opened during the disaster. Two safes that will still be full of valuables. There should be five million dollars worth of diamonds alone aboard the Titanic. Bringing out those vaults is the real purpose of Sterling's expedition. And it's our goal to get our hands on them."

"That shouldn't be too difficult," interrupts one of the men. "They won't be that heavily armed, and there's only a few of them."

Mortimer slowly turns his head toward the speaker, clearly not amused that he's been interrupted. "There are plenty of weapons on board," he says calmly. "The best of the best and enough to keep a small army going." These words impress the listeners.

"You don't know Sterling," Mortimer continues. "Firstly, he's a great lover of anything that fires; he has a vast collection of historical weapons in his home. When you meet him for the first time, you think he's just a friendly guy. And he is. But behind that smiling facade, there's a tough businessman. A friendly smile isn't enough to make you one of the richest people in the world. He's ruthless when it comes to achieving his goals, and he desperately wants those safes; and what he wants he gets. He had to approach a lot of people to organise the expedition. He probably realises his secret might leak out and uninvited guests like us might show up. For this reason alone, he'll have the necessary weapons to defend himself on board. Don't think it's going to be easy to hijack his ship. The Dutch professor has already experienced several adventures, so don't dismiss him too easily either!"

"How are you planning to get on board?" someone else wants to know. "If he has sniper rifles with him, we'll be under attack before we get anywhere close."

A faint smile appears on Mortimer's lips. "The Titanic crew thought she was unsinkable, and Sterling believes he's untouchable; both mistaken theories," then he taps his head. "There's a plan up here. A plan that cannot and will not fail. Mr Sterling and his expedition members have a little surprise in store for them, though sadly, one that will bring them very little pleasure; very, very little."

Chapter 6. A safe full of weapons

BOB AND ERIC are watching with interest the men who have gathered on the deck. The ship has just left the port of Reykjavik and is powering out to sea again. The last member of the expedition has come on board here, professor Magnussen, an expert in the field of conservation. His job is to ensure that the objects brought to the surface and documented by professor de Wolff will be correctly packaged and stored for the journey and preserved for the exhibition. There hasn't been a shopping trip at Reykjavik which disappointed Bob at first, but a quick walk round the city earlier made him realise that there isn't much opportunity for shopping there anyway. Nevertheless, they've just had the chance to take a short trip around the island. A few SUVs were hired for the group, and an experienced guide took them to an active volcano. They saw lava bubbling deep in the crater and a strange sulphurous gas coming up from the abyss.

On the return trip, they even saw a real geyser with hot boiling water spraying tens of feet into the air. The participants returned to the ship suitably impressed. "A diamond ring is beautiful, but I wouldn't have missed all this for the world," concluded Bob.

Bob and Eric are now sitting with their backs against the railing of the expedition ship. The Aquatic Dream is a large ship with every facility the crew and expedition members could need. It has a large flat stern which the Nautilus stands on. The Nautilus is a yellow submarine that can hold two people on board and dive to a depth of twenty thousand feet; it should have no problem reaching the Titanic which rests at 'only' twelve and a half thousand feet down. At the stern of the ship is a huge horseshoe shaped block from which the submarine is launched. The divers call it an A-frame as it looks a bit like a big A when the Nautilus hangs on it.

Eric sees his father approaching across the deck. The professor has just been sitting downstairs talking with his Icelandic colleague. Magnussen looks like a scrawny teenager next to the burly Dutch scholar, but the two men get on well together, connected by a common interest in history, especially that of the Titanic.

Soon, everyone comes up onto the rear deck. Sterling has gathered all the crew and expedition members together to tell them something important. The two professors, the two women, and Jessica stand among the divers and other crew members, the sailors, and the cook. Everyone is wondering what the billionaire is going to say. Bob and Eric are curious as well, but they don't go and join the group. Here at the railing they can see everything. Sterling leaves the bridge and stands at the railing of the upper deck. He looks at the men a few feet below him.

"The Titanic Expedition has now officially been launched," he begins. "Everyone's on board. You know our goal is to collect objects from the Titanic to make an exhibition, but above everything else, our aim is to find and lift the vaults. This means this expedition is not without danger."

The men look at him a little surprised.

"I prepared this expedition in secret," the American billionaire continues, "but once a secret has been shared by enough people, it risks being leaked. We have to be aware that criminal networks may come to know of our plans."

Professor Magnussen looks uncertainly at his Dutch colleague. De Wolff looks straight at the American, curious to hear what else he has to say. No-one is aware of Andy Howard looking away and swallowing. He is thinking anxiously of his wife and child at home and wonders if Sterling suspects that there is a traitor on board. He wished he never got involved in this expedition. Sterling continues his speech.

"I don't think anyone would dare to attack us in broad daylight and take the vaults from under our noses, but if someone proved to be that stupid, they'd be in for an unpleasant surprise. Let me show you something."

He leaves the railing and walks down the stairs to the lower deck. With a wave, he invites the men to join him. He's standing in front of a steel door which Eric notices has an electronic lock. "Behind this door is a surprise for any attacker," laughs the American leaning with one hand against the steel. He leans over the lock and taps in the secret code at high speed. Then he turns the wheel in the middle of the door; some clicking sounds inside and the heavy door swings open easily. René du Nord, the colossal diver, is standing closest and reacts excitedly as he sees what's inside. It's a room about ten feet wide and twelve feet long. Sterling puts on a light so they can all see. It looks like the warehouse of an arms dealer. Hanging closely together on the walls is a diverse range of weaponry: machine guns, M-16s, rifles, pistols and revolvers, even a mortar and grenade launcher. De Wolff stands shaking his head. For the first time he regrets ever volunteering for this expedition, but he goes into the room with the others. The American extravagance is evident even in here. There are so many weapons that they could have ten guns each, and it looks like the diving team would be happy to try their hand at it. They're already running around with their weapons of choice, though fortunately, nothing is loaded. Dr Reynolds doesn't look so happy, and neither does professor Magnussen.

"I wouldn't have a clue how to use any of this stuff," says Magnussen.

Overhearing him, Sterling slaps him on the back. "Then it's time to learn," he says.

De Wolff decides to speak up. "I don't know how to use one either," he says, "and I'm not going to learn. I'm on this expedition as a scientist, not a gunman."

Sterling shrugs. If he's angry, he hides it well.

"It's not compulsory," he says curtly, but de Wolff isn't finished.

"We certainly live in different worlds," says de Wolff. "Perhaps you thought I'd be happy to have a weapon to play with, but you're wrong. I'll do my job on board as a scientist, and I'll do it well, but I'm not going to shoot anyone."

Sterling purses his lips. He's not used to being spoken to like this, but he understands people well enough to know the Dutchman has made up his mind.

"Well, it makes no odds to me," he says, his manner friendly again. "I hired you as a scientist, and nothing more is required. I have enough real men on board who'll take up arms if needs be." He emphasises the word 'men'. "And I hope you're right," he says, before the professor can respond, "I hope we won't need to use them." He turns away.

Magnussen is in agreement with his Dutch colleague when it comes to Sterling's armoury and neither is interested in seeing more. After a short time, they both disappear below decks. But Eric and Bob come closer and peep inside the gunmen's Eldorado. They don't dare go all the way in, especially with René du Nord wandering around inside, although so far, they've not had much trouble with him. He seems to have accepted their presence aboard the ship. Sterling has now started a kind of tour.

"Here we have the lightweight Mitchell Guardian Angel," he says, lifting a rifle off the rack. "It's a big gun with a long barrel and a shoulder strap. For long distance fighting, we have this police weapon here. The Steyr AUG. A 9mm parabellum. It's deadly."

And so the billionaire goes on demonstrating his innate love of the weapons; he's a connoisseur. Eric and Bob watch him handle a diverse range of weapons, including rifles, carbines, and handguns. Some even emit a red beam to help you aim at your target: where the light falls, the bullet hits; you can hardly miss with such technology.

"Wow!" whispered Bob. "I didn't even know those things existed."

But the best is yet to come. Sterling bends over and with some difficulty lifts a hefty gun from the ground. "This is the best toy we've ever had on board," he says, his voice taking on a macho tone. "Let's just take it outside for a moment." Bending a little under its weight, he drags the almost twenty pound weapon to the rear deck. There's a large metal box on deck with a flat steel lid. Once its three legs have been set up, the weapon sits perfectly on it, and Sterling pulls out the foldable butt to its full 53 inches. "This, gentlemen, is the Harris M-93 Sniper!" he says with pride. Bob and Eric come closer.

"A sniper is a long range rifle," says Eric softly.

Sterling takes a few balloons from his pocket and a couple of men from the diving team blow them up before throwing them into the sea.

"We'll stop the ship in a moment, and I'll show you what this weapon's capable of," says the billionaire. The sea is as flat as a mirror, and the red balloons are clearly visible floating on the grey-blue water. Sterling gets a pair of binoculars and gives the man on the bridge a signal. The Aquatic Dream's speed slowly diminishes, and by the time she's stopped, the balloons can only be seen through the binoculars.

"This weapon is designed to hit targets at least one thousand yards away; it's so simple that a child could use it," Sterling continues.

He's interrupted by a disbelieving René du Nord. He points at Bob. "Let him shoot it then," he says defiantly.

Sterling is momentarily taken aback but recovers immediately. He glances at the door professor de Wolff disappeared through and then beckons the two boys over.

"Are you up for it?" he asks.

"Sure," says Bob, who has no intention of losing face in front of the French divers. Moreover, he'd love the opportunity to shoot with such a weapon. Eric wants a turn too. Sterling puts a box of cartridges beside the weapon with the words "50 BMGs" printed on the side. He digs out a cartridge and lays it on his hand before taking the opportunity to show off a little more of his extensive knowledge.

"This bullet was designed in 1921 by John Moses Browning, a famous weapons designer. It was meant for the Browning fifty calibre machine gun. BMG stands for Browning Machine Gun. It's a heavy cartridge which has a huge force on impact." He helps place Bob into position behind the weapon, and Eric moves in closer. Sterling shows them how to remove the magazine, load in the bullets, and put the twenty round magazine back into the gun. He devotes a lot of attention to explaining how the telescopic sight works and to helping set it up for Bob.

"Just look through the eyepiece," Sterling instructs.

Bob looks and sees nothing but water. He moves the gun round slightly, and suddenly one of the balloons comes into his sights. It appears to be so close that he can even see the knot it's been tied with, as if it were only a few feet away. A grid in the sights allows him to aim more easily at his target. Fortunately, the sea is calm and the balloon is barely moving. Bob's finger closes round the trigger.

"You can't shoot just yet," laughs Sterling. "The weapon is secured. Also you need to put the butt against your shoulder. The tripod will absorb some of the recoil but not all. Some of the impact will be on your shoulder. Push firmly against the stock and it won't hurt."

Bob adjusts to a better position behind the weapon and pushes his shoulder against it firmly.

"This is the safety catch," says Sterling. "Push it down with your thumb like that."

Bob clicks the lever down, cocks the gun, and the weapon's ready to fire. He takes a minute lining the balloon up in his sights again and then pulls the trigger. The weapon spews out fire and Bob gets a punch on the shoulder. He clenches his teeth. Beside him there's a cheer from the men as Sterling indicates it's a hit! René du Nord leans over and slaps Bob on the shoulder. "Très bon, mon petit, très bon," he says, and for the first time, Bob feels some warmth towards the huge Frenchman.

Eric looks at Sterling. He's also desperate for a chance to shoot. The billionaire gives him a nod, and Eric gets behind the weapon. But before he gets a chance to look through the sights, he hears a voice from the deck. A familiar voice. Father's voice. Having come up to see why the ship has stopped, the professor is now marching angrily in their direction. He's not at all happy to see his youngest son behind the weapon. Bob can't contain himself.

"Dad!" he exclaims. "I shot the gun! I hit a balloon a thousand yards away!" He demonstrates with his hands how small the balloon was.

But the professor doesn't seem to hear him. He's reached Sterling.

"Don't let me see that again!" he says angrily to the American, "How you mess around with your weapons is your business, but I forbid you to involve my children."

"But it's amazing!" says Bob, "Try it just once if it's okay with Mr Sterling!"

"Stay out of this!" his father reprimands him. "I want you to leave right now."

Bob says nothing, but there's fire flashing in his eyes. He turns and strides away with hunched shoulders. Eric scrambles quickly out from behind the weapon, disappointed that he's lost his chance to shoot and follows his brother. Moments later, they stand side by side at the railing looking down.

"So annoying!" Bob grumbles in frustration.

"At least you got a chance to shoot!" says Eric. "I'm the one you should be feeling sorry for."

"Your brother is an accomplished marksman, little boy!" Bob grins at him.

"I will treat you with more respect," Eric mocks his brother before punching him light-heartedly.

"Having fun?" asks a voice behind them.

The boys turn and see Andy Howard standing behind them. Bob and Eric don't know him very well. He's a quiet man about thirty years old who prefers to stay in the background. A bit of a loner. He doesn't fit in with the macho diving team, but he doesn't seem comfortable with the professors either. He spends his days surrounded by computers in the crammed radio room.

"I've just fired a sniper rifle," says Bob proudly.

"Dad wasn't overly happy about it," Eric continues. "That's why I didn't get a turn."

Andy nods understandingly. "Wanna take a look at the radio room?" he asks.

"Yes! Definitely!" Eric jumps at the chance enthusiastically. Bob nods too.

Moments later, they step inside Andy's domain. It's a bit like stepping inside a spaceship: computers from floor to ceiling; flashing lights; radar monitors with circular green lights.

"Wow!" Eric exclaims, the gun momentarily forgotten. "What's this?" he asks pointing at one of the monitors.

"That's the chart plotter," explains Andy. "It works using the global positioning system, GPS, to show us where we are. This device tells us, to an accuracy of within ten yards, where we are in the world; a bit like your car navigation."

"How far is it to the Titanic?" Eric wants to know next. Andy pulls one of his paper charts over.

"We're currently about here," he says, pointing at the map. "The Titanic is here. Look, I've marked it with a red dot on the map. It's about four hundred miles off the coast of Newfoundland."

"How long will it take to get there?" asks Bob.

"We'll be there by tomorrow I think," replies the radio technician.

"That's quick!" says Eric. "Are there icebergs there now?"

"No!" laughs Andy. "The Titanic sank in the spring, on the 15th of April. As the temperature rises in spring, the icebergs break off the polar caps and drift south with the Gulf Stream along the US coast. Now, in summer, the icebergs are long gone. No, we don't need to worry about icebergs!"

A shadow suddenly crosses his face. It's something worse than icebergs they have to worry about, although he still doesn't know exactly what. He quickly pushes the thoughts aside and concentrates again on the kids. It's good to have someone to talk to. He's been keeping his distance from the adults, afraid that they might start to suspect him.

Eric listens enthusiastically as Andy explains some of the electronic marvels surrounding them. After half an hour, Bob has had enough and says his goodbyes. All that stuff doesn't interest him. Instead, he watches the diving team from a distance; they are now shooting with the Harris M93. Sterling doesn't invite him to join them; the professor apparently made his point very clear. Bob watches a little jealously as René du Nord looks through the sights.

Meanwhile, Eric is having a great time. He gets on well with the American, and although some of the English words are tricky, he's managing to pick up instructions about how the various devices work. The one he's most keen to try is the radio. Andy's made contact with other ships a couple of times to show him how it works. On the radar, they can see where the ships are located. The nearest one is about sixty miles south. They tell the radio operators of the other ships that they're on board a cargo ship on the way to Newfoundland.

"Mr Sterling has asked me to avoid using the ship's name where possible," he says conspiratorially. "The Aquatic Dream is a fairly well-known expedition ship; when they hear we're in the vicinity of the Titanic, they'll guess what we're here for."

Eric spends the whole afternoon in the radio room and only leaves when he's called to dinner.

"Would you mind if I came again?" he asks the friendly radio operator.

"No problem," Andy assures him. "This is a lonely job, so you're always welcome."

Eric's back again after his meal. It's only when the professor comes to get him at ten o'clock that he reluctantly abandons his station.

Andy waits until exactly midnight. Then he locks the door of the radio room just in case of unexpected visitors. With a deep sigh he takes his place at the radio set and tunes in to a little used frequency. Almost immediately, he hears back from one of Mortimer's men.

"What's your location now?" the voice wants to know.

Andy checks the GPS and gives the exact coordinates.

"Any other useful information?" says the voice.

"Yes," whispers Andy. "Mr Sterling has a huge stock of weapons on board."

"We know," replies the voice, much to Andy's surprise. "Can you give us details?"

"No," says Andy, "I don't know, but there are a lot; a whole room full. They tried one of the guns out on the deck, and it shot a balloon a mile away. "

"That's not a problem," replies the voice. "Keep us informed." Then they're gone.

Andy puts his head in his hands. If they're not daunted to hear of the number of weapons on board, what scale of attack are they planning? He feels sick. It takes him a long time to fall asleep that night.

The radio operator from Mortimer's gang shuts down the radio and picks up the phone. A moment later, he has Mortimer himself on the line.

"I have confirmation that there are weapons on board," he announces.

"As we expected," Mortimer smiles. "It's easy to keep one step ahead when one knows exactly how Sterling thinks. He may be an avid chess player, but this is one game he's going to lose. Even if he had all the weapons of the US military on board, it wouldn't help him."

The next day Andy's pleased to see the Dutch boy showing up early again. Andy needs a distraction, and Eric is genuinely interested in the equipment. He soaks up everything Andy tells him, like a sponge, and Andy does his best to teach him as much as possible.

"Does every ship have a radio room like this?" he asks.

"No!" replies the American. "A radio room is really old-fashioned. Most ships have satellite communication equipment on the bridge. They've got one on our bridge too, but we have this room because of all the other equipment here: the sonar and the monitors for the underwater cameras for example. Most of this stuff is on the bridge too, but I can work undisturbed here."

"Wow!" says Eric admiringly. "If the Titanic had had this stuff, they'd never have hit the iceberg."

"Probably not," Andy admits. "They did have radio, but it only worked using Morse code. It was so modern in those days that it was seen as more of a toy than anything else, and there was certainly nobody regularly stationed at it. When the Titanic sank, there was another ship — the SS Californian — no more than ten nautical miles away. The radio operator had gone to bed ten minutes before the Titanic sent out their distress signal. If he had gone to bed fifteen minutes later, they'd have been able to rescue everyone off the Titanic before it sank. The distress signal was picked up by the Carpathia because the operator was a friend of the wireless operator of the Titanic and wanted to see if he was sleeping yet. The Carpathia went to the aid of the Titanic immediately, but it took them four hours to reach the scene of the accident by which time, almost everyone in the water had already died of hypothermia. Only six people were pulled alive from the water. Other than that, only those who got a place on a lifeboat survived."

"Do we have enough lifeboats on board?" Eric wants to know. Andy laughs.

"Sure," he says.

"Do the lifeboats have radios?"

"Yes and no," Andy says, a bit mysteriously. "It works a little differently. Each ship has an emergency radio on the bridge, wrapped in a waterproof box and stored in a marked cupboard. If the ship has to be abandoned, the captain or first mate takes it with them into the lifeboat."

"Do we have one on board?"

"Yes!" says the American.

"And then what do you do in the lifeboat?" Eric asks excitedly, his imagination all fired up.

"Make an emergency call," says Andy. "Each ship's radio is always open on the emergency frequency 2182. If you make a distress call on that frequency, they'll find you."

"Can we try it?" Eric says enthusiastically.

"Are you crazy?" Andy says. "What's the emergency?" But then he smiles.

"The radio on the bridge should be tested occasionally. If you go to the bridge and call me, we'll know it's working."

"At frequency 2182?" Eric grins.

"No!" Andy laughs, "We'll have to agree on something else."

"2110," says Eric, "October 21st is my birthday."

"Okay," says Andy, "you've learned a lot from me here. Let's see if you can use what you know to get the radio working. I'll be interested to see if you can manage it."

Eric is already away, sprinting to the bridge. He finds Sterling and the first officer there. The billionaire looks a little annoyed as Eric bursts in. He doesn't mind the kids coming along on the expedition, but they shouldn't be getting in the crew's way.

"What are you doing here?" he asks.

"Andy told me to test whether the emergency radio is working."

"Of course it's working," growls the billionaire. "It's not cheap junk we've got on board."

Eric hesitates a moment; he didn't expect any argument. But the first officer speaks up for him.

"It's standard procedure, sir!" he tells Sterling. "The radio must be routinely tested."

"Do you know how to do it?" Sterling asks, a little less fiercely.

"Andy explained it to me, sir!" Eric says politely.

"Well, show us then!" says Sterling.

Eric looks around for a marked cupboard. Before he can locate it, the first officer points it out. Eric runs over, takes out the waterproof box, and places it on the table. He opens it and takes out the radio. He's feeling a bit nervous with Sterling's eyes on him, but he does his best not to let this show. He takes a minute to look it over, unconsciously clicking his tongue, and then he switches it on. He puts on the nearby headset with microphone and turns the frequency knob.

"Have you done this before?" asks Sterling, a note of admiration in his voice.

"Not with this device, sir," replies Eric. He tunes in to frequency 2110 and sends a simple message.

"Andy, this is Eric! Andy, this is Eric! Over."

He jumps a bit when he hears Andy's voice in his headset.

"Eric, this is Andy! You're loud and clear. Out."

"Yes!" Eric yelled. "It worked!"

"Well done, son!" praises Sterling. "It's not a bad thing to learn the emergency procedures. Maybe it will come in handy one day."

Chapter 7. Into the abyss

THE YELLOW SUBMARINE, Nautilus, dangles like a fish on a rod in its hoist. Last night, they reached the place where the Titanic rests. On the sonar, it was possible to see a few spots which to a layman wouldn't have meant anything, but an expert could distinguish the bow of the unfortunate ship. As they stopped the Aquatic Dream, they made use of her dynamic positioning system, the DPS, to ensure that the ship remained on the same spot. The waters were too deep to drop anchor.

It is stunning weather for diving, and the divers have been spending a good part of the night getting the Nautilus ready. René and Albert are about to embark on a short test dive to see if all systems aboard the Nautilus are functioning properly, and if that goes well, they will descend to the wreck. Slowly the hoist lowers the submarine into the water, with Albert and René already aboard. As soon as the Nautilus is in the water, they navigate away from the large vessel to avoid a collision. Four other divers are already afloat in a dinghy. They are wearing flippers and have big steel bottles of oxygen on their backs. They head for the Nautilus and when they reach her, they put their mouthpieces between their teeth and plunge backwards into the water. What they're doing underwater isn't visible from the ship. After a while, the Nautilus drops several feet underwater, and there is nothing more to be seen from the decks. The watchers head up to the bridge, but even on the monitors there is almost nothing to see other than the occasional diver swimming by. There is radio contact with the men in the submarine, but the fast French exchanges are difficult to follow and the kids lose interest.

Bob and Jessica stretch out on the upper deck for some sunbathing. The weather is fabulous, not a cloud in the sky or a ripple on the water. Eric heads to Andy's radio room to pass the time. Together they listen to the divers' radio conversations and keep an eye on them on the monitors. After trialling the submarine for an hour, the divers conclude the vessel is ready for her first dive. Heavy cages are lowered into the water and sink to the bottom. The plan is not to try and fill them at this stage, but simply to see how far the currents will carry them away from the wreck. The cages have pockets attached to them which the submarine is able to fill with compressed air using a robotic arm. When they are full, the cages will rise naturally to the surface.

"There they go!" says Andy to Eric. Andy seems to follow the French conversation easily.

"How long will it take them?" Eric wants to know.

"It'll be almost three hours before they're down," Andy replies. "You can see them if you watch this monitor."

Together they keep an eye on the slowly descending submarine while Andy translates the cockpit conversations for Eric.

The three hours creep by, and on board the Aquatic Dream, a tension develops that increases the nearer the Nautilus gets to the bottom. When she's finally close enough to the wreck to start sending back images, everyone assembles on the bridge to watch the larger screens. Attached to the front of the submarine is a camera the divers call Robert. Robert is actually a tiny submarine in its own right, connected to the Nautilus by a long flexible cable. Its size allows it to enter areas the Nautilus couldn't fit through — a porthole for example. At the moment, Robert only sends out a green-grey image, just sea water illuminated by spotlight. Occasionally, bubbles and a few curious fish pass by proving that the camera is actually transmitting.

Suddenly, there's a cheer from the bridge as they see the seabed on the monitor. As Robert hangs a couple of feet above the sand, René du Nord contacts Andy to confirm the position of the Nautilus and the direction the wreck is in. They're quite close: the bow of the RMS Titanic is only about a hundred and fifty feet away. The viewers can see sand and small pebbles, and then suddenly, there's a cry from Sterling. He points to the monitor, and the others see it too. A plate. There's a dinner plate on the sea bed, proof that they are near the wreck.

And then, they see the ship! A wall of steel comes into view. The shipwreck looks like it's melting as long icicles of rust have become colonised by communities of bacteria which slowly eat away the ship's iron. The Nautilus begins to rise, and on the bridge of the Aquatic Dream, everyone falls silent. They're all looking breathlessly at the monitors. They can clearly see the rivets which keep the steel plates in place, at least where the steel wall is not overgrown with marine life. What a height the ship is! A huge steel hulk of almost a hundred feet!

The top of the bow comes into sight. The steel point is covered in debris to such an extent that its shape has been reduced to a round bulge. It is still clearly identifiable though. Eric recognises the railing from his book about the Titanic. The five bars are still completely intact, along with the grid beyond them and the massive chains lying on top. Further along, the railing is damaged, and the curved metal is covered in a brown coloured sludge. The Nautilus rises higher still, and then her lights are turned on to further illuminate the deck. They can see the whole area now: the majestic bow and railing, the deck stretching beyond it as far as the camera lens can reach. Eric feels a shiver go through him thinking of the terrible scenes played out on the now silent deck. Here frightened passengers ran in panic fleeing to the lifeboats. It was rumoured that the ship's band played hymns on this deck — such as "Nearer my God to Thee" — until the very end when the ship finally disappeared into the waves.

The Nautilus moves slowly forward, and they can see the remnants of where the bridge used to be. There Captain Smith stood with his hands behind his back and his teeth clenched —

perhaps thinking of his youngest daughter — until the rolling waves blew the windows in. There is almost nothing left of the upper sections of the ship: the wood is nearly all gone. "It's disappointing that so much of the ship has disintegrated," thinks Eric. It had previously been thought that, due to the low-oxygen environment, everything would be preserved. You can see clearly on the monitor that this has not proved to be the case, and it's one of the reasons why Sterling doesn't have an issue with salvaging what he can. In another fifty years, there might be virtually nothing left to save. The yellow submarine powers further on, and suddenly, the bow of the ship disappears from view as the submarine moves on to look for the stern.

René moves Robert some thirty feet above the seafloor. The amount of debris that can be seen is unbelievable; it's as if a warehouse has been turned upside down and shaken empty. Everybody watching the monitor screens is enthralled. There! A piece of staircase! A pillar of the ballroom! A suitcase! Cutlery! A full stove! Chunks of coal scattered everywhere! Then one of the engines comes into sight; it's as big as a four-storey building. The Nautilus moves slowly round it, and the words "Napier Brothers" are visible on a round plaque — the name of the engineering company that constructed these behemoths.

"There is one of the cages!" calls professor Magnussen. "It seems that the cages have ended up in just the right place which will save a lot of searching."

Their coordinates are quickly recorded. After a short time, the submarine reaches the stern of the Titanic, and they can peek deep inside just where the ship split apart. At the bottom, slowly rotting away, are hundreds of bags that belonged to the passengers. Slightly higher up are the cabins, and a bathtub can be seen protruding out from one of them. Next, there's the stairwell, but the enormous glass dome that originally covered it is gone. The Nautilus ventures a little closer wanting to see behind the captain's cabin where the massive vaults should be. They would be happy to start searching for them immediately, but this is a test dive, and moreover, the objects within easy reach should be collected first. The vaults will have to wait a few more days.

René lets the cable holding Robert out to its full extent so Robert can access the huge staircase. The gilded chandeliers, now covered with debris, slide into view on the monitors. Robert continues on, and the banisters become visible — a splendid example of the then ultramodern Jugendstil art nouveau.

"We'll need to get hold of a piece of that handrail," says de Wolff. "Of course, there are loose pieces on the bottom..."

Mrs de Wolff stands with her arm around Jessica watching as the Nautilus pulls back and moves once again along the devastated cabins. An expensive-looking perfume bottle left behind by a passenger lies under one of the sinks. "Did the owner survive?" she wonders.

"So many stories!" whispers Jessica, deeply moved.

"Yes," agrees her mother, "it's hard to imagine."

The group on the bridge have been so captivated by the images on the screens that they are surprised to discover they've been watching for two hours. It's long enough for the Nautilus' first dive and the rest of the day will be spent comparing the new images with all the existing photos and video. The professors now have work to do deciding what the divers should bring up. De Wolff must determine which pieces have the most historical interest, and Magnussen needs to assess what can be effectively preserved. Sterling is keen to contribute to the discussion and has a good sense of what the public will find interesting. At the previous exhibition, a jar of olives proved particularly popular. Olives are food and therefore a reminder of people's humanity which is perhaps more evocative than a piece of railing. A railing reminds people of the ship, but the jar of olives is a reminder of the people who were on board. The cook may have owned them and put them away in one of the lockers, the same cook who a few days later would be dragged down to the depths of the sea.

Bob and Jessica listen in for a while, but the discussion becomes too complicated for them, and they prefer to watch the submarine coming up. The Nautilus is surfacing a long way from the Aquatic Dream to avoid a collision. The dinghy goes straight out to help, and after some wrestling with cables and winches, the yellow cocoon is pulled dripping from the water and can be hauled aboard. The two divers are greeted with applause.

Soon nearly everybody is at work; Dr Reynolds examines René and Albert, a standard procedure after each dive; the dive team takes care of the Nautilus and prepares her for the dive tomorrow; the professors study the images; only Mrs de Wolff, Jessica, and the boys have nothing to do, but that will be different tomorrow as the first cages of objects from the Titanic will surface.

That night, Andy sends a short message. "First test run made to the wreck. Salvage work begins tomorrow." The answer is also short. "Keep us informed, especially about the vaults. End of message."

Chapter 8. The salvage begins

JESSICA LOOKS AT the stunning chandelier with admiration. The framework was designed to be capable of holding twenty lamps, and four of the originals are still in place. Some of the gold plating has gone, but you can still see how incredibly beautiful it must have been. The divers picked it up this morning — with the robotic grabbers from the Nautilus — and put it in the float cage along with dozens of other items, including a couple of traditional Dutch plates called Delfts blauw. The chandelier's gradually being restored, but this morning it was still covered in slippery grey seaweed. Professor Magnusson taught Mrs de Wolff and Jessica how to wash the different objects. Every cage that is brought up is emptied and the items placed in containers filled with seawater before being treated one at a time. Magnussen has all kinds of cleaning agents with him. First, he determines what substances should be used, and then the cleaning can start. Some items are cleaned up quite easily, but the chandelier has occupied four people for a day now. Before it's finally placed in the exhibition, it must be treated again, but that is a highly specialised job and will be done by Magnussen and his colleagues in a laboratory. Professor de Wolff is also admiring the chandelier and points to some of the curly looking decorations. "That style was very popular at the time," he explains. "Have a look at these pictures! You can see the same patterns being used on the bars of the banisters. The Titanic was decorated by clever artists with plenty of creativity. It was going to be the flagship of the Blue Star line, the company who owned the ship."

In the week that follows, the team dive every day, except for Sunday when they have a day to rest. They've already brought a couple of hundred objects to the surface, including many things of historic interest, but Sterling isn't satisfied quite yet. Professor de Wolff watches the monitors along with the divers, giving instructions on what items need to be lifted. It's hard though. Sometimes, objects are smaller or larger than they initially look. "It's just impossible to see what an item really looks like on the image feed we get," professor de Wolff complains again.

One evening, Sterling has a proposal for him.

"If you were to go in the submarine, you'd have a much better idea of what's on the bottom," Sterling says. "I've talked with the diving crew; there is room for two people on board; René du Nord is a very experienced diver and can control the submarine alone; he's agreed to you joining him."

De Wolff's heart thumps with excitement at the idea of having the Titanic just a few feet away, but he has to remember his family.

"How big are the risks?" he wants to know.

Sterling takes him to René du Nord for an answer. "Well, I'd be lying if I claimed that it's without risk," the French giant says. "The pressure on the Nautilus is about seven thousand pounds per square inch down there. Fortunately, the hull is constructed so that it can withstand the pressure easily, the windows alone have ten inch thick glass. Once we're down, we'll go between the front and back sections of the ship where the chances of us getting stuck are low. I'd say the risks are low for this trip; salvaging the vaults, where we have to go in and out of the wreck with the Nautilus, is much more dangerous. But you have to realise that if something happens, there's nobody who can reach us to rescue us."

The professor nods his head in understanding.

"I'll get back to you later today," he promises them, then leaves to look for his wife. He finds her cleaning silverware from the Titanic with Jessica.

"Can we talk, Elise?" de Wolff asks.

They find a quiet corner and de Wolff explains professor Sterling's idea.

"Do you want to go, Willem?" she asks when she's aware of the plans and the risks.

"It would be a challenge but one I'd like to take on," says de Wolff, "but if you think it's too risky, I won't do it."

Mrs de Wolff doesn't answer straight away. The chances of something going wrong are clearly small, but the descent is still risky. She doesn't want to think of what might happen to her husband, but she decides not to allow this to affect her decision.

"Do it!" she says, keeping her tone light.

The next morning, the professor takes part in a strange ritual. Each new diver must be initiated, and professor de Wolff is invited to appear on deck in full uniform — the yellow suit of the Nautilus. Then all the divers that have dived before with the Nautilus break an egg over his head. Supported by loud cheers from his three teenagers, the professor undergoes this delightful ceremony. Smiling, he sweeps the yolk from his hair and picks off a piece of eggshell between his forefinger and thumb. After a bucket of sea water is poured over his head, he's reasonably clean again. De Wolff washes off the lingering smell of the egg in the shower, and then gets ready for the descent. He climbs through the small hatch in the hull of the submarine. You couldn't do this if you had claustrophobia; there's not much space. The professor sees that there's a much better view through the round portholes then there are from the images fed back to the monitor. He tingles with excitement when the crane lifts the submarine from the deck, and moments later, water splashes against the windows as the Nautilus plunges into the sea.

René starts the engine, and aided by the diving team, navigates away from the Aquatic Dream. De Wolff feels sweat on the palms of his hands, owing to the stuffy atmosphere in the submarine, or perhaps due to nerves. René checks all systems and finding everything in perfect order, he starts the descent. The submarine dives slowly. At first, the water is bright blue, and they can clearly see the divers who guide the ship down for the first part of the journey. It gets darker soon after. If the professor leans forward a bit, he can look up through the glass on the roof to see a faint blue haze, but even that disappears a few minutes later. The headlights of the submarine light up the water for Robert so that its camera can film their surroundings. There is nothing but pitch black darkness all around them. Only the depth finder is an indicator that the Nautilus is actually travelling deeper. De Wolff tries to make himself as comfortable as possible in the narrow space. René is constantly monitoring the instruments, but he still finds time to chat. He was unable to understand why the professor made such a fuss about the weapons, but now that the professor is a 'member' of the Nautilus team, he has a new respect for him, and the three hours of dive time pass quickly as they talk. The conversation slows once they drop below ten thousand feet as René is fully occupied. He's in constant radio contact with Andy who can see on his equipment how close they'll be to the Titanic when they reach the bottom. He thinks they'll probably end up somewhere on the port side, and this proves to be correct when a dark shape looms out of the hazy light cast by the Nautilus.

"We're close," René says. He aims the lights straight ahead, and de Wolff moves forward to get as close to the glass as possible. The view is breathtaking — much more impressive than on the monitor back on the Aquatic Dream. The huge port anchor hangs just in front of them, half in its hawsehole. What a monster! You can see the colours clearly. What looks like brown sludge on the monitors actually has colours varying from yellow to dark red. The Nautilus manoeuvres slowly around the huge anchor and the professor is unable to take his eyes off it. As the submarine slowly navigates upward, the hand rail comes into view. The professor can observe it through the glass panel at the front of the Nautilus, and he follows it all the way to where it disappears beyond the misty light. The Nautilus embarks on a journey across the deck, navigating past the square windows of the cabins that were meant for the first class passengers. One of the windows is wide open, the glass still intact, and the professor can make out the rough outline of a bed. Further on, they see the two huge cranes that hoisted cargo on board.

René turns the Nautilus on the foredeck and descends to show his Dutch companion the huge hole in the side of the wreck. Was this damage caused by the iceberg, or by a coal-dust explosion? Or was it only damaged when the tons of steel and wood hit the bottom? It's guesswork. After an hour — and that's much too soon in the professor's opinion — they move to the seabed between the two sections of the ship.

With the lights on all sides, de Wolff finally gets an impression of what's down here: a wide range of all sorts of items. De Wolff knows he's been taken aboard to find the best pieces within the chaos, and René is looking at him expectantly. The professor tries to focus through the glass, but unfortunately, virtually everything is covered with a thin layer of sand making it hard to tell. Objects that look interesting turn out to be less special then anticipated when the arms of the Nautilus lift them from the bottom, and the professor realises that the opposite will also be the case. Still, he manages to find a few nice things — a beautiful piece of carved fencing, a copper pan, the oven door of one of the furnaces from the kitchen, and a beautifully carved chair that probably stood in one of the salons. Then, suddenly, he sees something that could turn out to be the showpiece of the collection: a sculpted head looks at them, and de Wolff recognises it from the pictures. It's one of the sculptures that stood in the second class smoking, a woman with a raised arm holding up a lamp.

"Can you pick it up?" he asks René excitedly. "The statue is buried at least three feet into the sand."

"I can try," the Frenchman replies simply. He manoeuvres the gripper arm towards the head and the woman smiles kindly and allows herself to be strangled by the arms of the Nautilus. René pulls the Nautilus up, but they soon come to a stop. The Frenchman increases the upward pressure, and in a cloud of sand, the statue slowly loosens from the soil. The Nautilus rises sharply when the sand suddenly surrenders its hold, and the statue comes loose. Terrified, de Wolff tries to grab on to something, but René doesn't even flinch. Carefully the Nautilus brings the sculpture to one of the collection cages, and using Robert, they are able to show everyone on the Aquatic Dream what they've found. Sterling is excited, a showpiece! This could be almost as big a hit as the vaults.

The hours at the bottom of the Atlantic fly by, and all too soon, it's time to go up again. The bright lights illuminate the area around the yellow submarine one more time, and de Wolff quickly takes a last look at the indescribable chaos on the ground around them. In the distance, de Wolff can make out the outline of one of the engines — a mysterious mountain. Then, the Nautilus breaks free from the bottom, and in the blink of an eye, what remains of the Titanic disappears from view. There is nothing more than ocean water around them. On the depth finder, the professor can see that going up is a lot faster than going down, but after the excitement of working at the bottom, it feels like it takes longer. When the water in front of the windows begins to dawn blue, the end is in sight, and suddenly, there is Albert's face peeking inside. Back and forth the thumbs go up. The trip is over. The professor is glad when he comes out of the narrow hatch fifteen minutes later. Smiling, he lets the waves of questions roll over him. Sterling appears to be very satisfied; the findings of today surpass all those of the previous days.

"Tomorrow we will attempt to salvage the vaults," he says. "So far, everything has gone smoothly, and we're going to have the same luck with the vaults. I can feel it."

That night, Andy Howard sends another message. "The search for loose items is complete with the most impressive items being brought up today, including a beautiful statue. Tomorrow, the search for the vaults begins. End of message."

The message is received by an extremely satisfied Mortimer aboard the Rubicon. He sits in a leather swivel chair, elbows on the armrests and fingertips touching. "Time to take action, gentlemen!" he tells two of his bodyguards, "Give the men aboard the Swordfish the signal we agreed on. The time has come to head in the direction of the expedition ship." He launches himself energetically from his swivel chair and walks to the bridge. He finds his captain there. "It's time," he says. "Has everything been brought on board?"

"Yes, sir!" the captain replies.

"And the men aboard the Swordfish, do they have their equipment?"

"They have everything they need on board, sir!"

"Fine!" says Mortimer satisfied. "Make sure that we're ready to leave within an hour! I don't want to be far away if they find the vaults."

An hour later, the Rubicon moves away from the shore. Slowly she navigates through the Port of New York. After they pass the Statue of Liberty, they set sail on the Atlantic towards Newfoundland. They are travelling in the direction of the final resting place of the Titanic, in the direction of Sterling's expedition ship.

Chapter 9. The vaults of the Titanic

"I'LL SEND IN Robert," René's voice can be heard over the speaker.

Everyone has been staring anxiously at the monitor since the search began. Three hours ago, the Nautilus disappeared under the water, and now, René sits in the submarine in the wrecked stern of the Titanic. Alone. This time it's really dangerous. The Nautilus could get stuck on something, and if René fails to get her free, he is doomed. René carefully manoeuvres the submarine to the ruined staircase, and then, extremely cautiously, he descends between the pillars of the handrail and into the belly of the ship. Two floors down is the main lounge which is accessible now thanks to one of its walls having rotted away. Once inside, the submarine is completely enveloped within the ship. A startled, strange looking fish swims away through one of the portholes. The photos showing the vaults were taken near the captain's cabin. René knows where he should go — Robert entered the ship from the outside when those photos were taken, but the vaults can't be extracted through the side wall of the vessel — he will have to go through the lounge and the stairwell. The vaults were previously positioned in a corner, but he wonders whether they will still be accessible. René cruises slowly on. He pushes aside a couple of tables and chairs. The sand rises up and forms a cloud, and everything looks spooky with the long dirt garlands on the walls and furniture — an extraordinary and eerie decor. The gilded pumps show over the edge of the bar which is still partially intact. The mirror behind it is broken but still in place, and René sees the reflection of his own submarine gliding past like a yellow ghost.

Suddenly he sees them! One of the vaults is still in its original location — a massive steel giant spanning five feet long. As he gets closer, he sees that the other vault fell straight through the wall and into the captain's cabin. It looks like a fallen cupboard. No wonder it wasn't recognised immediately. René adjusts Robert's camera so that everyone on the Aquatic Dream can see the vaults. He knows everyone's eyes are feasting on the sight of the vaults when he hears their enthusiastic screams and cheers through the speaker.

There soon follows a discussion about how the vaults should be brought to the surface. The Aquatic Dream is equipped with a twenty-thousand-foot-long steel cable which has already been lowered to the bottom. René will have to try to attach a karabiner to the lock wheel on the vault door. Using the monitor, Andy guides him to where the cable hangs. With great care René powers back through the stairwell, and using the arm of the Nautilus, he picks up the cable hook from the soil. Up on the deck of the Aquatic Dream, they let the winch feed more cable so René can move back inside, and for a second time, René makes the dangerous journey into the bowels of the ship.

Half an hour later, the Nautilus is positioned right next to the overturned vault. This vault must be removed to make way for the other one. René realises his palms are sweaty. He carefully lets the gripper holding the karabiner glide forward, and once it is above the wheel of the vault, he releases the cable. The karabiner falls between two of the three spokes. The arm picks up the cable and cautiously pushes it a little further so that the karabiner emerges from under the wheel. Now comes the difficult part - the cable that's been dropped through the wheel must be picked up and connected higher up onto the cable again so that a loop is formed. Everybody on the Aquatic Dream follows René's efforts on the monitor. "Bad luck, you almost had it!" and similar comments are made whenever the hook slips off the cable. René fails over ten times. And then suddenly, the karabiner clicks around the cable - the fish is on the line! Now all they have to do is reel it in.

But first, René needs to get out. The Nautilus slowly slides backwards towards the stairwell. René is just starting to relax when a shock judders through the submarine. Startled, the Frenchman looks out of the window. What happened? He is right in the middle of the staircase, and he's confident he didn't hit any of the railings. Carefully he tries to make the submarine rise, but the only thing that happens is that the Nautilus moves off to the side, away from the steps. He must not get stuck here. He quickly stops the engines and forces himself to keep calm. He tries to see what's going on through the windows, but he can't see anything unusual. Carefully he starts the engine again and tries to move upwards, and again the Nautilus travels sideways. How is that possible? He looks through the glass again. He can see the steel cable connected to the vault; could that be in the way? He requests over the radio that the winch is fed some more cable. He can see it's been done when the cable that was tightly strung through the stairwell falls limp. He tries again to move the submarine, and this time she slips neatly up and then out of the Titanic. "Start pulling," he instructs, and immediately the cable is pulled tight. Will the one centimetre thick steel cable be strong enough to pull the heavy vault from the wreck?

Up on the Aquatic Dream they've started to make preparations. The vaults can't be put on the deck because as soon as the water drains out of them the contents will be ruined. The vaults must remain filled with water until they are opened by an expert, and Sterling wants to wait until there is maximum publicity before this is done. In order to keep the vaults wet, they've constructed containers on the deck. They're made of thin steel walls that can be hooked together to form two small watertight pools. These containers will be filled with sea water, and then the vaults can be laid in on their backs.

The strong winch increases the tension on the cable which is now worryingly taut. Sterling won't allow anyone to stand near the winch in case it suddenly comes loose. It strains as the cable is reeled in inch by inch.

René can see the taut cable running into the wreck, but he doesn't know if the vault is moving. One of the handrails bends under the pressure of the steel cable. Then suddenly, red-brown clouds of sand form. It looks as though the vault has moved through the lounge and is now dangling in the stairwell. If only it doesn't get stuck now! The Frenchman sees a corner of the vault, and the monster emerges slowly from the wreck. It's unlikely anything will go wrong at this stage; if the cable was strong enough to pull the vault from the lounge, it will certainly be strong enough to lift the heavy steel box to the surface. Delighted, he indicates through the radio that it's on its way up.

On the Aquatic Dream, the preparations for the vaults are now complete, and the diving team is already waiting in their boat alongside the cable. They will attach an extra cable to the vault when it appears, as once it is above the water, it will be even heavier. A pair of divers are already in the water and are the first to see the monster slowly surfacing from the darkness. They swim towards it and guide the steel case on the last few feet of its journey to the surface. The extra cable is lowered and secured on to the vault. This time it's not just attached to the wheel on the door but tied round the whole unit. The others can see everything clearly from the bridge, and Sterling has his camera out to record this historic moment so that later — at the exhibition — the public will be able to follow the story of how the safe was extracted. The vault is lifted with caution and placed safely on its back in the pool. Water sloshes over the edge. The cables are disconnected, and everyone draws nearer to see the monster up close. What's hiding inside this steel cabinet? No doubt, a lot of money — bundles of notes which have lost their value but will still be a crowd puller at the exhibition — but the vault might also contain the gems that were left on board.

De Wolff has less interest in the vaults. Frankly, he doesn't think they are the main finding, and the exhibition is not the reason why he came on this expedition. He finds the other objects much more interesting. They help paint a picture about what life was like in the period when the Titanic was made. He also hopes the exhibits, if they do take place, will help visitors understand that humans are not infallible. They may have built a huge vessel thought to be unsinkable, but it only took one mistake to turn all that glory to nothing but a heap of twisted steel on the bottom of the ocean.

Meanwhile, the cable with the karabiner attached has begun to descend to the bottom again. René still has a few hours of time underwater and they are going to try and pick up the second vault. Everything seems to be coming together today. The hook lands almost beside the Nautilus, so René can pick it up immediately without a search. With the cable in the claw, he heads back to the stairwell and realises the second journey is going to prove difficult. The cloud of sand created by the first vault still hangs like a fine mist in the stairwell. René knows the way, but he sees that the cable has warped a banister. It's quite possible that the steel vault has caused other damage on the way out, for example, there could be a banister completely ruined and hanging like an invisible net in the stairwell, ready to entangle the Nautilus. René is not a man to let his imagination run away with him, and he powers on moving a little slower than the first time he descended into the wreck. He sees — through a fine mist of sand — the entry into the lounge, and although several tables and chairs have been pushed out of place, it looks like there's nothing to worry about. A brown trail shows the path left behind by the first vault, and this serves as a handy guideline for René. Despite the limited view in the foggy lounge, he finds his way back to the correct corner, and the second vault appears in his lights. The Nautilus bumps into a corner of the bar as it makes its way towards the vault, and the rotten wood breaks off as if it were made of cardboard. Reaching the vault, the robotic arm clenches the cable in its claw. This time, gravity is in René's favour as the karabiner drops effortlessly behind the wheel. René makes a loop around it, and after a few unsuccessful attempts, he successfully clips the hook back onto the wire. The safe is attached; René can leave the ship and head towards the surface. Slowly he navigates his way back. He hits a few tables or chairs in the sand-filled lounge which create a hollow thud in the submarine. Without further delay, he makes his way out of the wreck. He has plenty of time to assess whether the second safe will be successfully dragged from the Titanic. The cable tightens as the huge winch on the deck of the Aquatic Dream relentlessly pulls the steel vault through the lounge and staircase towards the surface. René sees it coming out of the wrecked stairwell and then starting to slowly travel up. He focuses Robert so that everyone on the Aquatic Dream can also see what's happening down below. Then he takes the Nautilus on its upward journey; the final dive of the expedition is almost over.

There is fevered activity on board as the second vault is hoisted onto the deck with great excitement. Nobody notices Andy sitting alone in his radio room. He's been told to make contact once the vaults are recovered. With trembling hands, he turns the controls on the radio feeling like a despicable traitor. In addition to his guilt, he is fearful of what will happen next. How will the criminals take possession of the ship? Will they bring death and destruction? Will they see him as the inconvenient witness that he is, or will they let him live? But the only thing that's important to him right now are the lives of his wife and daughter; it's them he has to think of first. With that in mind, he sends the following message: "Salvaging of the vaults has exceeded expectations. Both vaults are already on board. End of message."

Mortimer looks at the satnav to check where the Rubicon is located.

"We'll never make it in time," says the captain, worried.

"We will," replies Mortimer calmly. "Don't forget that Sterling will set sail towards us. Besides, he won't leave before tomorrow morning — he'll have a party on board tonight. Anyway, the crew of the Swordfish still need to do their work. How far are they from the expedition ship?"

"About a hundred nautical miles, sir."

"Then they'll be there around sunrise," Mortimer says. "That's soon enough. We'll arrive in the afternoon, but by then the ship will have been in our hands for some time, and the treasures of the Titanic will be mine."

No one is aware of these plans aboard the Aquatic Dream, and just as Mortimer predicted, there is indeed a party. The cook is doing his utmost to produce enough food and drink. The only one who is not in a celebratory mood is Andy. He's been watching a dot that has been on the radar for some time now. It must be a ship and it's now about eighty nautical miles away and getting closer. It will be here by morning. Should he warn Sterling? The billionaire will probably see nothing to worry about as they're not far from a busy shipping route, and eighty nautical miles is still a long way away. Yet as Andy continues to watch, he can see the distance getting smaller by the minute.

Chapter 10. Modern piracy

"WHY DID YOU wake me up so early?" Sterling growls. It's been a late night, and he's not happy to find Andy phoning him at six in the morning.

"I think you might want to join me in the radio room, sir!" replies the radio technician. "It's important."

Sighing, the billionaire places the handset back and groans as he gets out of bed. Quietly, so as not to wake his wife, he pulls on his dressing gown and slippers and heads to the radio room. "What is it?" he barks.

Andy points at a circle of green light on the radar screen. Sterling doesn't see anything significant straight away, but then he notices a small bright spot. "Hey," he says, "a ship in the vicinity?"

"Yes, sir, about eight nautical miles away."

The billionaire shrugs. "These are international waters," he says, "anyone can sail here. Is that all you woke me up for?"

"I've been watching it all night, sir, and the ship has been heading straight for us. I find that very strange. He points to a small dot on the edge of the screen. "Here's a second ship," he says, "and it looks like she's heading this way too."

Sterling lowers himself into one of the leather swivel chairs. "Can't you get radio contact with them?"

Andy shakes his head. "Believe me, sir, if anyone here understands marine communications, it's me. I'm sure they can hear me on the frequencies I'm using. I've tried to get in contact with them all night, but they're not responding and that's a violation of international protocol. At sea you identify yourself; every skipper does. Unless he has something to hide, of course," he adds.

Sterling is suddenly much more interested. "Strange. Is it a big ship?" he wants to know. "I mean, if they were pirates planning to attack us, then it would have to be a good ship, right?"

"That's what's so odd," says the radio man, "because if you believe the radar, it's a very small ship."

"Keep trying to get in touch!" Sterling commands. "I'll take some precautionary measures; it's better to be safe than sorry."

He heads down the stairs and disappears into the bowels of the ship. He stops when he reaches René's cabin and knocks on the oak door. A few moments later it opens, and the sleepy head of the French giant looks out.

"There's a ship heading right for us," Sterling says.

"Do I have to wake the whole crew?" René wants to know.

Sterling thinks for a moment but then shakes his head, "Let's see what's going on first," he decides. René pulls on a pair of jeans and a sweater, and the two of them head up onto the deck where Sterling goes straight to the armoury. "We'll set up the sniper rifle," he says. "We'll be able to see through the scope who's coming towards us, and if it proves to be a threat, we'll have plenty of time to warn the others."

Without waiting for René's reply, he taps in the secret code and pulls open the weighty door. René steps inside, takes out the heavy weapon, and sets it up on the deck.

"Where's the ship?" he asks.

Sterling puts his fingers in his mouth, whistles loudly, and Andy appears.

"What direction is the ship in?" the rich American wants to know.

Andy takes a look inside the radio room and then indicates a point on the horizon. "It's somewhere over there."

René looks intently in the direction Andy pointed, and then kneels behind the weapon and peeks through the scope. There's a light morning mist on the water. Slowly he moves the circle of the scope across the horizon seeing not much more than a white haze. Then suddenly, there's a black shadow. René adjusts the sights so his view is clearer and catches a glimpse of a ship coming right at them. "I see it!" he shouts excitedly. Sterling looks in the direction the barrel is pointing in but sees nothing. Andy, who is a few feet higher, can't see anything either. Suddenly, they hear René cursing softly.

Professor de Wolff woke up when Sterling whistled for Andy. He looks at his watch with his eyes half open. "Six-fifteen?" he murmurs. He hears firm footsteps on the deck above his head, and suddenly all thoughts of sleep are gone. Being careful not to wake his wife, he slips out from under the blankets and quickly puts on a pair of slippers. He cautiously opens the door of their cabin, slips into the hall, and soon he's greeted by the fresh air coming in from outside. It's still early and quite cold, and the professor shivers in his thin dressing gown. He walks along the corridor and emerges on the back deck. To his surprise, he sees René lying behind the sniper rifle looking anxiously through the scope. Suddenly, the giant Frenchman jumps up and tells Sterling to come closer, and the billionaire kneels down to look as well. Curious, the professor looks in the direction the barrel of the gun is pointing in. At first, he can't see anything through the morning mist that hangs over the remarkably flat sea, but then his eyes pick out a dark dot. Could that be the top of a mast? He holds his hand up to his eyes for a better view. What's coming towards them? Another ship? After a few minutes he can see exactly what is calmly advancing towards them.

Eric can't sleep. He's usually a light sleeper, and the footsteps on the deck have woken him up. Beside him — in the narrow cabin — Bob is sleeping as deeply as a bear in winter. His breathing sounds like a cheap coffee maker. A bit irritated, Eric punches him, but Bob just responds with an extra loud snort and then turns away. Eric throws off the covers and jumps into his jeans. After pulling a sweater over his head, he puts on his shoes and makes the decision to go look for Andy in the radio room. He climbs up an internal staircase to the corridor where the radio room is and knocks on the door, but there is no reply. He looks at his watch: six-twenty. Andy would normally have been working for a while. Eric knocks on the door again, and he is once more greeted with silence. He opens the door carefully and peeks inside. All the radio equipment is on: the lights flash and the microphone is ready. Eric sees that the door leading outside is open, and he sees Andy staring anxiously over the railing out to sea. Curious, Eric comes closer and stands alongside the American.

"Good morning!" Eric greets him smiling broadly.

Andy seems startled and turns to him with a frightened expression but recovers himself quickly forcing a thin smile to his lips.

"Hi!" he responds and then turns immediately back to sea, the worried expression back in place.

Eric looks out in the same direction, and just as he sees a ship sailing towards them, he overhears René saying loudly, "It's just an ordinary fishing boat. What a waste of time!" He can't understand why the American appears to be so anxious. He looks down at the lower deck and sees René heading back to the armoury with a big rifle.

"Ah," Eric snorts with laughter. "Sterling probably thought it was a pirate ship flying the skull and crossbones with a couple of guys with wooden legs and eye patches all ready for battle. They obviously prepared the gun, and now it's turned out to be nothing more than an ordinary fishing boat."

To his surprise, he sees that Andy isn't smiling along with him. Instead, he grabs the young Dutchman by the shoulders and looks straight at him. "There's definitely something not right with that ship," he says hurriedly, "stay here with me in the radio room."

"What makes you say that?" Eric asks, a little dazed.

"They won't make radio contact," the American replies.

"Maybe their radio is broken," Eric suggests, but Andy shakes his head. "Why don't you tell Mr Sterling if you're worried?" he goes on.

"I can't," Andy cuts him short without further explanation.

Andy turns away from the railing and steps inside the radio room before emerging a moment later with a large pair of binoculars. He holds them up to his eyes and stares at the black fishing vessel. With the naked eye you can already see some men at work on the deck. Sterling is also peering at the ship through a pair of binoculars on the lower deck wondering if Rene is being too complacent, but when the other ship starts to turn, he decides he's seen enough and puts them away.

Andy doesn't. He remains watching intently as if at any moment he expects something terrible to happen. Eric feels the tension. He looks into the radio room and spots another pair of binoculars on the table. He hurries in and grabs them and then stands alongside the American and looks for the ship. At first he sees nothing but water, but then he catches sight of the boat and the men working on the deck. What are those guys doing? It looks like they're assembling something. With a little imagination it could be a small cannon. Would they be able to shoot harpoons with that?

Suddenly, he hears Andy cry out beside him.

"A mortar!" he yells. "They have a mortar on board!" He runs over to the railing and shouts down, "René! René! Look at the ship!"

René has just finished putting away the gun and with a firm movement pushes the vault door closed. He turns around and looks at the fishing vessel just in time to see a missile lifting into the sky leaving a whimsical plume of smoke as it flies in their direction.

René instinctively throws himself on the deck and covers his head. Out of the corner of his eye he sees the Dutch professor dive under the stairs. Andy looks with bewilderment at the rapidly descending arc of smoke. Eric rushes inside, afraid of a huge explosion. Images of the sinking Titanic flash through his mind. Will their ship be shot to pieces? Will they sink? Are they soon to be resting at the bottom of the ocean alongside the Titanic? Through the panoramic windows, he sees the projectile racing towards them. It smashes on the aft deck and then rolls towards the radio room. Eric cowers, expecting a thunderous explosion accompanied by flying glass and twisted metal, but there's no explosion; just a dry bang like a firecracker on a New Year's Day; then suddenly, there's smoke, dense white clouds of it rising up in the air, and Andy hurls himself inside slamming the door shut behind him.

"I think I understand what they're planning," the American whispers in a panic. He grabs Eric and looks at him, eyes bright with adrenalin. "We're done for," he gasps.

Chapter 11. The Robbery

RENÉ SLOWLY UNCOVERS his ears as he realises that the explosion he's been waiting for hasn't happened. There's a cloud of smoke rising a few yards away from him, and he looks with surprise at the white mist.

Sterling rushes out to the deck beside him. The billionaire was making his way inside when he saw the missile heading in their direction. Now he yells loudly, not out of fear but to wake up the rest of the crew. They're actually under attack. He strides with determination to the vault door which hides his armoury. Some of the smoke hangs in the air in front of it but Sterling ignores it. Apparently the enemy wants to impose some kind of smoke screen on the ship. Ha! Let them try. Some of the guns are equipped with infrared scopes that the smoke won't interfere with. If they want a fight, then a fight is what they're going to get.

As he extends his fingers towards the keypad on the door the white smoke penetrates his nostrils, and he immediately detects the odour. At the back of his mind alarm bells are ringing, but he continues opening the vault door. As he reaches for the steel wheel, he suddenly has the feeling that he's moving at an astonishing rate as if he's on a rollercoaster. It lasts for a split second, and he sees a flash of blue sky before everything goes black, and then nothing.

René sees Sterling collapse. He looks suspiciously at the white mist which is slowly spreading across the deck. He hears another thud behind him as a second shell finds its target. René tries to figure out exactly where it's landed and decides it's somewhere up on the foredeck. It would seem that the intention is to smother the whole ship in smoke. But why? Is it really just a smokescreen? Did Sterling collapse from stress or does it have something to do with that smoke?

He quickly lowers himself as a smoke cloud travels towards him. He wriggles on his belly towards a door leading inside while trying to pull his handkerchief from his pocket. Before he reaches the door, the smoke catches up with him. He presses his lips together. He has managed to get hold of his handkerchief, and with the small piece of cloth clamped to his nose, he staggers in. He slams the door behind him and leans back against it panting heavily. He realises too late that quite a lot of smoke has come in with him. There's a stinging in his throat, and he quickly clasps the handkerchief to his nose. The whole corridor starts to shift in front of his eyes. Determined to stay upright, he drunkenly zigzags down the hall, opening his mouth to alert those who are still sleeping. Before he can make a sound he drops to his knees. He tries to push himself back up, but the last thing he remembers is his head coming crashing down onto the thin carpet which does little to soften the blow.

Professor de Wolff takes shelter under the stairs when he sees a missile coming. It explodes close to him, and pieces of steel shrapnel miss him by a hair. Then the white cloud floats in his direction, and even before the professor has a chance to come out from behind the stairs, the acrid smoke penetrates his nostrils and he's flat on his back.

Andy and Eric are temporarily protected inside by the closed door.

"What's happening?" Eric asks anxiously.

"They're going to take over the ship," the American says decidedly.

"Who?" Eric wants to know.

"A criminal organisation," Andy replies. "A group of tough guys, they'll stop at nothing."

"How do you know all this?"

"Listen to me!" Andy says, silencing Eric with a gesture. "We haven't got much time. I have to tell you something, and then I'll hide you. Maybe you'll be able to escape them, and then at least someone will know what's happened."

Questions crowd into Eric's mind, but he keeps quiet and concentrates on what the radio technician is saying.

"I don't know exactly what they're planning," Andy begins. "They broke into my house right after I pledged to go on this trip. I don't even know how they managed that because my house is well protected. They wanted to force me to work with them. I didn't want to, of course, but after they kidnapped my wife and later my daughter, I was left with no option. They threatened to murder us all if I didn't cooperate. My job was to give them regular updates over the radio. I told them yesterday about the vaults being lifted from the wreck. As soon as I saw a ship on the radar heading this way, I could only guess what was about to happen. I tried to warn Mr Sterling, but when he finally took action, it was too late."

Eric is shocked. Andy, a traitor? It just doesn't make sense, but the American has told him himself. After what he's heard and what he sees outside, he realises Andy isn't lying. "We must warn the others!" he cries, but Andy shakes his head.

"It's too late!" he says decisively. "We won't be able to defeat them anyway. I've seen them in action, and I know how effective they are."

"What are they going to do with us?" Eric whispers. He's never been so scared, "Will they—"

Andy interrupts to try and reassure him, " — my wife and daughter came home unharmed. Their aim isn't to kill people; they just want the vaults and other valuables from the Titanic. They'll keep us hostage in some way, but you can still hide. A boy will not be missed, and they won't see you as a threat. You may get a chance later to free us. We have to use this opportunity! Will you help? "

All sorts of thoughts are flying through Eric's head, and he shrugs his shoulders uncertainly. "Uh, yes," he says, hesitantly.

Andy gets up and looks through the windows. There's not much to see as a grey haze of smoke now hangs over the ship. Then — like a shadowy ghost from an old legend — he sees the outline of the fishing vessel. It looks like they're planning to come alongside. There's no time to lose. He grabs Eric's shoulder, steering the boy over to the tables where the radio equipment stands. They have low cabinets under them, and Andy pulls one of them open revealing that there's almost nothing inside. He quickly moves aside the few folders sitting in the bottom of it. "You'll fit in here," he says. Eric looks at the narrow space; he probably will fit with his knees pulled up, but the thought of squeezing in there isn't very appealing.

There's a bump, and the ship rocks slightly. The fishing boat is banging against the Aquatic Dream as grappling hooks are thrown over and the small boat moors herself to the larger ship.

"Quick!" Andy gently pushes Eric forward. Eric squeezes into the cabinet and pulls his legs inside. Andy snatches the keys from the lock and hands them to him.

"You can lock it from the inside as well," says Andy, then shuts the door.

For a moment Eric can't see anything. He runs his fingers down the inside of the door and feels a tiny breath of air where there's an air vent. As his eyes adjust, he can see just a little light coming in. He leans forward and looks through the fine mesh to discover that he can see into the radio room. His fingers grope for the lock and push the key in. As he turns it, he feels just a tiny bit safer. A little fresh air is able to come in through the air vent. Looking through again, he can make out Andy standing at the window.

The radio technician is looking anxiously outside at the scene unfolding before his eyes. He doesn't like what he's seeing, and a cold fear is creeping around his heart. The deck of the fishing vessel isn't visible because it's lower than the deck of the Aquatic Dream, but he can see the bridge and the masts and then a hand clutching the railing. When the head rises above the railing, the American cries out in fear. The man is wearing a commando sweater and is wielding a flamethrower, but even more frightening is his face. Or rather the lack of his face. The intruder has a gas mask on, and the large reflective eye holes and shiny filter give the man the appearance of a giant insect. A second man, looking just as terrifying, also hoists himself up aboard the Aquatic Dream. The first man turns and sees the radio technician. Andy would like to run, but he's frozen in fear, and he simply stares as the man crosses the deck and enters the radio room. Andy automatically holds his hands up to his face as the intruder aims the flamethrower at him.

Eric is looking out through the air vent and sees the creepy guy come in looking like a monster from another planet. Eric clasps his hands to his mouth when the weapon is aimed at his friend. A dense cloud of gas is released in Andy's face almost as if a fire extinguisher has been let off. What is that stuff?

He sees Andy swaying on his feet. The American grasps desperately at one of the computer desks. Pulling a keyboard and a stack of papers with him, he falls between two swivel chairs leaving the white, nebula-like clouds still hanging over him. Eric sees the white vapour coming in his direction. The air vent! That stuff will come inside! What should he do? With some difficulty, he searches his pockets for a tissue. His position is not comfortable at all, and manoeuvring is not easy, but he manages to find a tissue. He's still looking through the vent at the guy standing in the doorway whose head is moving from left to right making slow work of checking over the room due to his gas mask limiting his vision. The gas rifle travels round with him, and for a moment Eric thinks it's stopped and is pointing at the cabinet where he's hiding.Eric stiffens but the man turns around and steps back out of the room. Eric quickly stuffs the tissue in front of the fine mesh just before the white mist reaches the door. His fingers are trembling. Will that stuff still get through? What is it anyway? Poison? He mustn't think about what might happen to his parents, Bob, Jessica, and the others.

What he can't see is that there are already five men equipped with gas masks on deck. According to their pre-arranged plan, they fan out across the breadth of the ship — apparently already knowing their way around — and move across the deck. They weren't expecting much resistance on deck after the gas attack, but inside it could be different. They enter the ship and methodically open every cabin. Most of the crew are surprised in their sleep, and a short blast from the gas rifle is sufficient to take them down.

Mrs de Wolff is awake and looking with surprise through the porthole. Mist? That's strange. The cabin door opens behind her and, expecting her husband, she turns round. She gives a scream of terror when a man wearing a gas mask enters, and in a reflex action, she grabs the blanket off the bed and swings it in his direction. The man is quite surprised but realising his vision is about to be momentarily impaired, he presses the trigger of his gas rifle. As the blanket lands, thick clouds of gas come out from under it. He pulls it off in time to see Mrs de Wolff's hand already going in the direction of the sheet, but the gas is too quick. There's a stinging sensation in her nose, a bitter taste in her mouth, and the room starts to dance around her. She collapses on the bed with her feet still on the floor. The man behind the mask makes a grunting noise. The sweat is running from his face, and his eye mask is clouding up, but he knows better than to take it off.

Jessica wakes when she hears a thud and a slight vibration passing through the vessel. What was that? They're not lowering the submarine, are they? She looks groggily at her watch: it's still early. She throws off the covers, puts on her slippers and walks to the porthole, sliding the flowered curtain aside. Hey, what's that? A steel wall in front of the window? It takes a few seconds before the truth dawns on her: there's another ship next to them. Who are they, and what are they doing here? She lowers herself down on her knees and turns her head for a better view. She sees the railing of the other ship, and a cross mast stands out against the bright blue morning sky — a mast with ropes like a fishing vessel. Then she sees a hand gripping the railing, and a dark figure pulls himself up, apparently planning to switch from one ship to the other. A split second later, she sees the man passing by with a gas mask on his face and a scuba tank on his back. Immediately her suspicions are aroused. This isn't just a fishing vessel; why would a fishing vessel come alongside in the middle of the ocean? No, this is more like a robbery. She must warn the others!

She hears a loud bang in the hallway as if a door has been violently slammed. With a jerk she opens the door of her own cabin and looks to the left as she sees something moving in her peripheral vision. René staggers drunkenly in her direction before sinking to his knees. The huge Frenchman starts to clamber back to his feet and then crashes to the floor. Jessica gives a shriek of terror. What's happening? She walks slowly towards the Frenchman who is lying on the floor like a sack of potatoes. Is he dead? As if in a dream — or a horrible nightmare — she inches closer, and then the outside door opens again and the nightmare continues. A man in black is coming in slowly. His face is covered by a mask, and on his back is a gas cylinder which is connected by a hose to some sort of gun. Jessica lets out a cry and runs back to her cabin. With a crash she slams the door shut, and her fingers fiddle frantically with the key. Someone grasps the doorknob and turns it as Jessica puts her shoulder against the door. The door opens a few inches, but she's able to push it back because the man isn't expecting resistance. She turns the key quickly and stands with her shoulder against it. There's a loud thud and a thump on her shoulder as the man throws his full weight against the door. He then kicks it repeatedly with his heavy boot, and she hears the sound of splintering wood. The doors of the Aquatic Dream weren't designed to withstand attack.

Jessica looks around desperately for something that could be used as a weapon but sees nothing suitable. She must hide. Where? Under the bed? No, that's too easy and too obvious! The wardrobe! She pulls one of the mirrored doors open, and pushing the clothes to the side, wriggles her way in. With her fingertips, she pulls the wardrobe door shut. There's a loud crack and then a thump as the lock breaks, and the cabin door literally flies against the wall. Jessica hears the man kick the bed to the side, and she squeezes her eyes shut. A moment later, the inevitable happens, and the wardrobe door is pulled open. Jessica looks out between two dresses at the guy. She can't tell whether he is triumphantly smiling, or if he is angry. The mask hides every emotion and that is perhaps the worst thing. Her assailant doesn't seem to be flesh and blood but a robot or a creature from another planet. The gas rifle comes up, and Jessica puts her hand over her mouth. She feels a faint irritation in her throat and then blacks out. Heavy boots move away back down the corridor.

Bob is caught sleeping just like Dr Reynolds. Professor Magnussen thinks he's dreaming of a scary creature entering his room, but a blast from the gas rifle puts an end to his nightmare. Fifteen minutes later, everyone on board has been 'put down.' The five men meet on the upper deck where the smoke has abated a little. The leader unfolds a blueprint of the ship which they stretch out on one of the lifeboats. Along the edges are pictures of every member of the expedition, and the leader wants to make sure they've all been taken down. The team split up and begin identifying people. René is found in the corridor, the Dutch professor under the stairs, Sterling near the vault, and Andy Howard in the radio room. When the exercise is complete, there is still one picture that is not crossed off. A boy. One of the sons of the professor.

"Are you sure he's on board?" one of the team asks the leader. "It seems unlikely we'd have missed him."

"He was going to come," replies the man, "and the other children are here. Why would they leave him at home?"

"Perhaps he chose to stay at home with a friend?" suggests one of the men.

"It'll be a while before the others are here," says the leader. "You search the vessel once more, thoroughly. I'll go to the radio room and report back that it all went according to plan."

The four others nod and step back inside the ship. The team leader lets the gas tank slip from his back and climbs the stairs to the radio room. He throws the door wide open so the gas can disperse, but most of it has already gone anyway. He could probably take off his mask, but he decides not to take the risk.

He lowers himself down on to one of the swivel chairs and shoves Andy carelessly aside with his foot. He flips a few switches, turns the knob of the radio, and then connects directly to the remaining men on the fishing boat.

"The operation went without problems," he says keeping it short. "Stay on board for the moment as there is still a lot of gas on the ship." His voice sounds strangely smothered beneath his mask. "I'm going to contact the Rubicon now. Out."

He tinkers with the radio again, unaware of two eyes watching him anxiously from a cabinet about a yard from his knee.

Eric does his best to make no sound. He's opened his mouth slightly because he thinks that breathing through his nose might be audible. Eric hears the man pressing the buttons on the radio, a sound he's become familiar with over the last few weeks. But the familiar atmosphere of the radio room is gone now that a stranger is using the equipment. There's a crackling from the speakers, and Eric can hear the man speaking as he tries to establish a connection, but he's not sure of what's being said. The man is speaking in code and also in English, though a word that keeps coming up is "Rubicon." Would that be a code word, or could it be the name of a ship? Suddenly, a voice can be heard over the speakers. Again, that word Rubicon. Eric gently leans forward so his ear is pressing closely on the door of the cabinet. He wants to catch as much as possible of the conversation.

"Is Mr Mortimer available?" the man in the mask asks.

A moment later, he has the great leader himself on the radio. "Mortimer here," says a cold voice. "How did the operation go?"

"Exactly according to plan," replies the masked man. "We fired gas grenades on board. There were already a few people on deck: Sterling, the leader of the diving team, and the Dutch professor. They went down immediately allowing us to couple the ships together without resistance. Once on board, we surprised most of the rest of the crew in their sleep."

"Nice," Mortimer's voice sounds satisfied, "and you've checked the list to ensure that nobody's been missed?"

The man in the mask hesitates. Should he tell him one of the professor's sons hasn't been found? He's not sure how Mortimer will react to a problem with the plan, however small.

"We're working on it right now," he says neutrally.

"Fine!" is the response from the speakers. "We expect to be with you by the end of the morning. Make sure everything is ready by then."

"No problem, Mr Mortimer!" The words sounds hollow coming out from the respirator. Then the call is disconnected, and the man sighs. He looks around and pulls up his mask a little. He breathes in gently and then holds his breath for a while. When it's clear he's not feeling dizzy, he pulls the stuffy mask from his head and rolls his chair back in relief. He sees something moving out of the corner of his eye. It's the others arriving back, and seeing him without his mask, they pull off theirs as well.

"Have you found the boy?" the leader wants to know.

"No," replies one of the other four.

The leader hisses a rude word. He thinks for a moment. "Do you have the blueprint with the photos?" he asks. One of the men takes it out, and the team leader unfolds it on the desk. It hangs down just a few inches from Eric's face. The leader grabs a pen and puts a cross through the picture of Eric. "Keep your mouths shut," he says to the others. "If we've been unable to find him, he's probably not on board, so let's not make an unnecessary fuss. We have plenty of other work to be getting on with." He folds up the blueprint. "Let's go!" he says, and all five of them leave the radio room.

Chapter 12. Eric stands alone

ERIC SIGHS WITH relief as the door of the radio room closes behind the men. He wipes his forehead with the back of his hand and realises he's sweating; it's very stuffy inside the cabinet. Through the vent he sees Andy and a cold shiver passes through the boy. Is his American friend alright? Is he still alive? If he's no longer alive, it doesn't look good for the others. Dad, mum, Bob, Jessica! He can't just sit in this cabinet. He has to know! He turns the key very gently and hears the lock mechanism moving. He carefully pushes the door open, and as he stretches a leg out, he realises how stiff he has become. It's as if his muscles are screaming. Ignoring the horrible feeling, he crawls out. There's no sign of the five guys. He crawls over to Andy — who is still on the ground between the two chairs — and finds to his relief that Andy isn't dead. A soft snoring sound escapes his chest. Eric puts his fingers on Andy's Adam's apple and pushes to the right into the carotid artery until he feels a heartbeat pulsing steadily. So the gas isn't fatal. It's only meant to knock out those on board. The crew will recover after a while, but what will happen in the meantime?

He is startled by a faint rumbling noise coming from outside and crawls over to the window. He peeks out carefully and sees two of the men at work nearby. They're casting off the fishing boat. The sound he heard was its engine. Their boat is leaving! Glancing round the deck of the Aquatic Dream, he can only see the two men. It looks as if the rest might be leaving with the boat. On the deck of the fishing boat, he can see some men dressed in the same commando sweaters the attackers worn. He's pretty sure it's the same guys. They pull the mooring ropes in and wave to the two men who have remained on board the Aquatic Dream.

With some power to the thrusters, the fishing boat loosens herself. The powerful engines turn the ocean water into foam. The bow rises up, and the boat powers away at speed. The two men left on the Aquatic Dream remain at the railing for a moment before exchanging a few words and disappearing into the ship.

Eric doesn't understand what they're planning. First they come aboard with a group to attack, and then, just when they have things under control, they head off again. How will the two men left on board the Aquatic Dream leave the ship? Or will they stay? If they stay, they're going to be in trouble as soon as the crew start to regain consciousness, though how long the gas will work Eric doesn't know. Could they be down for a day or two? Those guys could take the ship somewhere else within that time. They haven't gone to the bridge though so it doesn't look as if they're planning to move the ship. Then what are they doing?

Taking a deep breath, he stands up, but there's no sign of the two guys. He decides to stay in the radio room where he can hide again quickly if he needs to. He realises how lucky he's been. Apparently they've searched the entire ship for him but never thought to check the radio room. Sometimes you forget to look right under your own nose. Suddenly, he hears a knocking sound and automatically dives down. Realising it's not near the radio room, he sits up again and looks out of the window in the direction of the noise. It sounded like it came from somewhere on the back deck. One of the men appears carrying a crate in which valuables lifted from the Titanic have been stored. The man walks along to the large containers in which the vaults lie and puts the crate beside them. Eric can now see that the beautiful brass chandelier is in the crate. Then he sees the other man also carrying a crate, although he's too far away for Eric to make out exactly what's inside. It's stuff from the Titanic, that's for sure. Why are they taking it up onto the deck? Are they planning to throw it overboard? No, they would have done that immediately. There can be only one explanation: they're going to move the crates to another ship and steal everything! Then why didn't they take it on to the fishing vessel? Of course! It's too small to store the huge vaults on deck which means they must have a bigger ship. Could it be on its way already?

Eric quickly runs to the radar and turns the screen on. The revolving line casts a green fan around the screen, and as Eric stares at it he is unnerved to see a clear dot visible — a ship heading in their direction. Studying the circles, he sees that the ship is not far from them. It must be quite a big ship. How fast will it travel? He's pleased he's learned so much from Andy. He reckons it could move somewhere between fifteen and twenty knots an hour. Eric estimates the distance, looks at his watch, and does some quick maths in his head. He suddenly feels scared. It's not going to take them that long at all. They'll be here later today, and then what? He feels utterly alone. He's the only one who's not under the influence of the gas, the only one who knows what's going to happen, and he's the only one who has the opportunity to do something about it. He's also the only one who will have to shoulder the blame if he makes a wrong decision. For the first time, he wishes they'd drugged him too. He silently prays for help, for wisdom to make the right decisions, and he feels a little calmer. He's not entirely alone.

Sighing he turns in the chair. For now, he can't do anything. He just needs to keep a low profile. If those two guys see him, the game is over. But perhaps there will be a chance to do something after the other ship arrives. He looks at the radar screen. Even in that short time, the dot seems to have moved closer.

Later that morning, the Rubicon comes into view. Eric has been keeping an eye on the radar, and he's been observing the two men who are still trying to bring the treasures of the Titanic up onto the deck. Using the binoculars, he peers along the horizon where the water and the sky blend into one another.

Yes! There it is! A white glare in the distance! Eric shifts excitedly in his chair. What kind of a ship will it be? It is a few more minutes before he can get a better look at the vessel. A tall slim bow rises proudly out of the water. From the front, it appears to be a beautiful boat. He'll be able to see the rest if the ship comes around. It looks like the type of big yacht you'd expect a wealthy oil sheik to own — a brilliant showpiece with a large flat rear deck. That's probably where the vaults will be stored. From now on, he'll have to watch his step. If that ship comes alongside, more men will come on board, and the chances of discovery will be significantly higher. He decides to turn off the radar and opens the doors of the cabinet wide so he can dive right in if that should prove to be necessary. Then he can do nothing more than anxiously wait.

Mortimer is standing on the bridge of the Rubicon with his binoculars, taking in the Aquatic Dream. He says nothing, but a satisfied smile plays around his lips. He's outwitted Sterling and taken the treasures of the Titanic from right under his nose. He puts the binoculars on one of the tables and leans on the railing. Slowly, the Rubicon draws closer to the Aquatic Dream, and his men efficiently moor the two ships together. The sea is calm making the job easy. Hoisting the vaults aboard is going to be no bother at all if it stays like this. The Aquatic Dream's huge crane will put them neatly on the Rubicon's deck. Mortimer walks down the stairs to the lower deck and leaps over the two railings separating the ships. They are virtually the same height; the Rubicon has turned out to be a very sensible choice.

"Hi, Jerry!" he greets the leader of the assault team. "Everything went according to plan?"

"Sure, Mr Mortimer!" replies the man in the commando sweater. "The robbery was a piece of cake. Two grenades on the front and rear, and the rest was done with the gas rifle. We encountered virtually no resistance."

"Did you check the list?" Mortimer asks.

"Yes, sir!" replies Jerry.

"Good!" the gang leader sounds pleased. Then he goes to look at the back deck. He sees the vaults lying on their backs in the containers full of seawater. That's disappointing; he honestly didn't consider this possibility, but he understands why it's been done. Clearly the safes need to remain full of water until they're opened. They'll just have to take the containers on to the Rubicon, but it will require a lot of extra time.

"How long will these people be down for?" he wants to know.

"It depends on their body weight and the amount of gas they inhaled," says Jerry, "but I don't expect any of them to come round before midnight. Most of them will be back on their feet by tomorrow afternoon. They'll probably have raging headaches for the best part of the day."

"Hmm," growls Mortimer. "At midnight we'll be long gone, but there's a lot to be done before then." He puts his fingers to his mouth and whistles to summon some of the men.

"The safes need to be lifted," he says, "but they can't be removed from the containers as they need to remain in the water." The men look closely to assess the containers.

"We can take the containers apart," says one of the guys. "I think we'd best hoist the vaults out first, disassemble the containers, and then reassemble them aboard the Rubicon where we can refill them with seawater. Then we can lift the vaults to our own ship."

"That means that we'll have to hoist both vaults twice," reasons another man.

"I can't see another way to do it," says the first man. "If we try and hoist them while they're still in the containers, we risk the container coming apart and the possibility of the vault falling to the bottom of the ocean again, or smashing on the deck, and I wouldn't want to be around if that happens."

Some rapid discussion follows, but it's eventually agreed they have no choice but to take the containers apart.

Mortimer is now talking with a few others. "Have you got all the videos?" he asks.

"No!" says one of the men surprised. "Why do we need them?"

Mortimer shakes his head at their ignorance. "I'm going to sell everything that comes from the Titanic," he explains. "There will be plenty of potential buyers, but they'll need some evidence that what they're considering purchasing really comes from the Titanic and not from some scrapyard. We can only provide the evidence with the videos and paperwork."

The man nods his understanding. "I'll find it," he says. "We'll get on it immediately."

A number of crew members have now begun to lift the crates from one ship to the other. "Make sure you don't drop anything overboard," Mortimer calls to them, "every object is worth its weight in gold." The men signal they've heard, and the ringleader is satisfied. He walks round to the front of the armoury where Sterling is lying unconscious and looks down at him for a moment. "Checkmate, old boy!" he chuckles, then he turns and climbs back aboard the Rubicon. He doesn't see the pair of eyes watching him from the radio room.

Eric's still at his post. He's considered returning to the cabinet to hide, but the robbers have stayed on the aft deck continuing with their work as he predicted. Everything Sterling's divers have collected has been taken to the other ship. Stolen. The expedition has been for nothing. Of course, they can dive to the wreck again with the Nautilus, but the showpiece, the vaults, are all gone. He wonders who these people are. Andy talked about a kind of American Mafia, but he didn't seem to know much.

The young boy's tried to wake Andy up several times, but the radio technician just lies there like a sack of potatoes; so instead,

Eric's working on memorising the faces of the robbers, thinking that this may be useful information to have later.

Glancing out, he sees again, to his annoyance, that one of the vaults is being lifted from its container. They lower the colossal thing down a little and then begin taking the container apart. "Well, yes, take that too while you're at it," he thinks angrily. His eyes slide up to the bridge of the other ship, and he wonders if he can be seen from there. He wouldn't like to be discovered here now. He can see the tall fellow with the hard eyes. That must be the boss; he seems to be the one giving out the orders. Just to be on the safe side, Eric slides down out of view.

As the afternoon passes, Eric starts to get hungry, but he doesn't dare go out to look for food. Slowly, the sun starts to sink into the horizon. The men are down to the last vault and are getting it harnessed up. Everything's probably taken longer than they expected because of the extra work involved with the vaults. The twilight casts long shadows making it difficult for the men to do their job, and a bright light is switched on for them on the Rubicon.

It's at this moment that a plan unfolds in Eric's head. The light blinds the people working in front of it. Perhaps it would be possible to scramble up onto the other ship and stowaway on board. He would be able to see where the vaults were taken and then call for help! He immediately rejects the plan, way too dangerous. What if he was discovered, or they took the vaults somewhere where it was impossible to contact the police? But the idea has been sown, and it slowly takes root in his head.

Before long, Eric sees the last vault dangling in the hoist, the scene illuminated by the spotlight. It's almost dark now, and once this vault is aboard the other vessel, they'll leave. And go where? If he could only go with them to find out! Yet then he would lose contact with all the others, and he really would be on his own. No! Just the thought of it is scaring him. Of course, he doesn't necessarily have to lose contact with everyone; he could take the emergency radio with him! He could call Andy if he found a good hiding place. Even as he thinks this, he realises how dangerous it would be. If they found him, he'd be caught red-handed. What should he do?! Eric decides that while he's making up his mind, he could at least try and get the radio. He probably doesn't have much time left to make the decision.

The spotlights, four of them now, illuminate the sterns of the ships. It's unlikely that they'll see him. He opens the door of the radio room. It's cold outside, but after a whole day in the stuffy room, it's a welcome change. With his back against the deckhouse, he creeps round to the foredeck, but as he walks up the stairs, he sees to his disappointment that there's a light coming from the bridge. He expected the bridge to be unmanned. Carefully he climbs a little higher until he can see in through the bridge windows. Well, there you have it! There are two guys standing, talking to one another, each with a rifle hanging down his back. Forget it, he'll never get past them. Disappointed, he sits down on one of the big pipes to think. In a while, the guys will be called from the bridge to go back to their boat, but by then he won't have enough time left to grab the radio and to get aboard with them. His only chance to make the move is when the lights are on; once they go out, he'll be visible. What should he do?

The vault now dangles above the seawater container. The winch is being cautiously turned to allow the vault to be slowly lowered. He has another fifteen minutes at best; then everything is over. He should probably just be happy that they'll be leaving.

He can wait here quietly until the others wake up. No one will blame him for not doing anything. After all, what could he have been expected to do? Yet these thoughts don't satisfy him. He looks at the bridge of the other ship where there is only one man present. Wait! Would there be another way to do it? The other ship probably has some sort of emergency radio on the bridge too! Couldn't he get hold of that one? It's kept safe in a cupboard; it's not likely anyone would notice straight away that it was gone. He could contact Andy and guide the Aquatic Dream to the attacker's ship. A strange excitement tingles through him. It's risky though. What if there's no radio? What if he's discovered? What if he can't make radio contact with Andy? What if he can't figure out which direction the ship is going in? What if, what if, what if . . .

But sometimes you have to avoid overthinking things. He remembers Bob who does everything without any thought at all. Slowly Eric gets up, and goes back down the stairs. He walks along the foredeck until he's close to the Rubicon. There, in the bow, is a steel lifeboat with a hood over it; the perfect place to hide.

Eric ignores his growing anxiety and moves quickly to the railing. He grabs the steel bars, and with one quick motion he jumps up and swings his legs over. He's standing on the other ship! Sick with nerves, he crouches down and sneaks across the foredeck to the lifeboat. It's a solid, well-built boat covered with a plastic tarpaulin. Eric grabs the handle, lifts the tarp, and climbs inside. He tries to regulate his breathing; he could still back out now if he wanted.

The vault is lowered into the container on the Rubicon, and the large pulley swings back up. The lights turned to the Aquatic Dream are switched off; so is the light on its bridge as the gunmen withdraw. Some of the men are now on the foredeck of the Aquatic Dream making preparations to leave. Eric can see everything through the gap between the edge of the lifeboat and the tarpaulin. He can see one of the men untying a mooring rope on the Aquatic Dream just a few yards away. It would be impossible to get past now without being spotted. The thrusters roar to life pushing the two ships apart. The rope falls along the hull of the Rubicon as the two ships separate. The last man leaps from the Aquatic Dream to the Rubicon. He clings to the railing for a moment before swinging his leg over the edge and climbing aboard. A moment later, the distance between the two vessels is too wide to be crossed even with a jump. Suddenly, Eric regrets his decision.

But it's too late.

Chapter 13. Radio

THE FIRST HOUR in the lifeboat was the worst for Eric. The crew kept walking by and he was sure someone was going to pull back the cover and discover him, but nothing happened. After that first hour, things settled down on board and now it seems the crew have either sought entertainment somewhere inside the ship or have gone to bed early.

Eric is hugely relieved. He's seen that most of the crew are carrying guns and is increasingly aware that these are hardened criminals, but there seems to be nobody left on deck now except for the men on the bridge. Eric gradually relaxes; there isn't much he can do just now anyway. If he wants to reach the radio on the bridge without being noticed, he'll have to do it later on in the night. If this ship operates like the Aquatic Dream, then there will only be one man left on the bridge by then.

Since he can't get out of the lifeboat, Eric decides to take a closer look around it. He finds he's made a good decision. Along the sides are mounted benches with lids, and when he opens them he finds all sorts of useful things. There are food packages (enough to last for days), medical supplies, and a gun for firing flares, as well as blankets and life jackets. Eric lies down on one of the benches, puts a life jacket under his head, pulls a blanket over himself, and falls asleep.

It's the middle of the night when Eric wakes again; a glance at his watch tells him it's four-thirty. He doesn't know exactly when the sun will come up, but he realises it won't be long. Once the daily routine on board starts, he'll be trapped in the lifeboat again. If he wants to make a move, he'll have to do it now.

He slowly pulls the tarpaulin back from the lifeboat. He must be within view from the bridge, but the lifeboat is in a dark corner, and the bridge is lit up brightly. Eric swings his legs out and lowers himself onto the deck. It's cold outside, and he shivers in his thin clothes, but it's pleasant to be out in the fresh air. Still, perhaps it would be a good idea to look for some warmer clothing later. Staying low, he runs across the bow until he reaches the shelter of the deckhouse and he's no longer visible from the bridge. He enjoys the temporary feeling of safety. Right next to him is a ladder that will take him up near the bridge, but he's not sure what to do from there if the bridge is still manned. He slowly climbs the ladder and peeks over the top.

Sure enough there is someone there, but like a moth to a flame, he finds himself unable to resist drawing closer. He climbs on to the upper deck and hides behind some kind of chest. The man on the bridge takes out a cigarette. He flicks on his lighter, and Eric sees that he's a huge guy. He wouldn't like to fall into those hands. If he hoped to take the man out with a surprise attack, then he's in for a disappointment. What should he do? Light a fire as a distraction? Then the alarm would probably be sounded, and everyone would be on deck within five minutes. Suddenly, behind the man, he catches sight of a cabinet with stickers he's seen before on the bridge of the Aquatic Dream. There is a radio there! He has to do something, but he can't stay here all night lurking around in the hope that the man abandons his station for ten minutes.

He shudders. The cold is starting to take its toll on him. Maybe he should look for some warmer clothing first. Where would that be? He realises with frustration that any stores are likely to lie somewhere well within the ship. He doesn't dare to go inside; what if he accidentally walked into a cabin and woke a light sleeper, or perhaps happened upon someone already awake. Eric sighs. He can't think of anything to do except return to the lifeboat. He will just have to wait until they reach a harbour.

Eric turns back to the ladder and climbs down. Just as he's about to head for the lifeboat, he sees a steel door further along the deck. He gathers up his courage and moves towards it. It's probably just a corridor; he can't see a porthole or another window. He reaches the door in three steps, grabs the steel handle and gently pushes it down. It's not locked! Carefully he opens the rather heavy door and slips inside. At first he can only see darkness, and feeling around, he almost cries out in alarm as his hand touches fabric. There's someone there!

His fears subside when the fabric moves aside at his touch; it must just be clothing that's been hung up. He feels his way along the side of the room until his fingers find a light switch. He almost puts it on, but then he realises the light might be visible to the man on the bridge. He closes the door and then turns on the light. He's afraid of what he might see, but fortunately there's no one there. He's standing in some sort of stock room; there are overalls, waterproof suits, boots and ropes hanging up. There is bound to be something warm he can use here. Further in he sees a rack of sweaters, the dark commando ones the robbers wore. One of those will do nicely. He quickly looks at the labels until he finds one in his size and pulls it over his head. Fits like a glove. Now he needs to get out of here quickly; he's been wandering around long enough.

He turns around and then stops suddenly. Leaning against a couple of benches are the gas rifles. That's the solution! If he stunned the man on the bridge, he could get to the radio! It's a pretty dangerous plan. He won't be able to hide quickly wearing the gas tank, and he'd need to take good care not to bump it on anything. He lifts one of the tanks onto his back; the weight isn't actually too bad; he goes to pull the trigger to test it and then stops, realising that if he releases the gas here, he'll knock himself out. How can he tell if it's ready to use or not? That's another problem! But there's no time to think about it, and so far everything has gone quite well. He looks around for a gas mask but can't see any. Actually, he doesn't mind. He doesn't like the idea of having the stuffy mask over his face, and it must be hard to see through the small eye holes.

Cautiously he opens the door and looks around. Nobody else seems to be up yet, but he needs to hurry now. He sneaks back along to the bridge and climbs the stairs being careful not to bump into anything. When he reaches the top, he pauses to think. The bridge is accessible on both sides by a door, but the man is in the middle, several metres from either door. It's not possible to get in unnoticed. Of course, he should be able to take the man out fast, but when the guy comes to his senses, he'll remember he was attacked, and they'll search the vessel. Eric is under no illusions; he knows they would find him easily. There are large panoramic windows at the front of the bridge; he must stay away from those. However, at the rear of the bridge, the windows are higher up, and there are air vents under them. Maybe they'll provide him with the opportunity he needs. Moving closer, Eric sees that the air vents are at about knee height, and to his delight, he realises that they're open. He slowly lowers himself down, and biting his lip, slides the gas rifle inside. His finger rests on the trigger. He takes a deep breath to avoid breathing in any gas and squeezes. Immediately a cloud of gas escapes the barrel. Eric only holds the trigger briefly, and the hissing noise is negligible. As far as he knows, the man hasn't noticed anything. Eric's lip hurts from where he's been biting it nervously, but this is going pretty well. The gas cloud descends, and the man suddenly crumples down onto one knee. He tries to grab a lever in front of him, but before he can reach it, he sprawls sideways onto the floor.

Success! The man probably didn't even realise what just happened to him. Now Eric's determined to finish his mission. He quickly makes his way round to the door, throwing the gas rifle and tank overboard on his way. They are too bulky to move about with on the bridge, but losing them overboard may not be such a bad move. When the man on the bridge recovers or is found by someone, they may just assume he was unwell. If there's a gas rifle nearby, they'll know immediately what's happened. He takes a deep breath, holds it, and opens the door of the bridge. The man is snoring gently on the floor. Eric opens the cabinet, tears open the box, and there's the radio. He's getting desperate to breathe, and he slowly lets some air escape through his nose to take some pressure off his chest. He snatches the device from the box, and starting to feel dizzy, he staggers to the door. As he walks out something catches his eye, but he can't stop to look now, he has to get out. Once outside, he leans over the railing and greedily crams his lungs full of fresh air. For a brief moment he feels a little lightheaded. Did he inhale some of the gas? As the floating feeling disappears he places the radio down, takes another deep breath, and looks inside the bridge once more. Yes, he saw correctly, one of the gas rifles has been left there. If he leaves it lying on the floor beside the man, it might look like it's been set off accidentally. After stepping out for another deep breath, he goes back inside and knocks the rifle to the ground. He glances at the SATNAV to check their position so he can communicate it to Andy. The things Andy taught him are really coming in handy now! He hurries back out, and with the radio under one arm, he sneaks back to the lifeboat. He can see the sky turning a little blue already. Climbing back into the lifeboat, he flops down on one of the benches with a sigh of relief. So far he's been successful, although he still feels uneasy. What will happen when the unconscious man is found? He tries not to allow his mind to fill with questions. The first thing to do is to try to get in contact with Andy which is easier said than done.

If he gives any information over the emergency frequency 2182, anyone can listen in. But if he radios through on a different frequency, Andy won't hear him. He pulls on his lower lip, thinking. Wait! The solution suddenly comes to him. When they tested the radio on the Aquatic Dream, they used his birthday as the frequency. That's how he should do it! For now he can just try to establish contact over the emergency frequency. The guy on the bridge should be out for a while anyway.

Quickly, he puts on the headphones and tunes the radio to the emergency frequency. In a low voice he says, "Eric to Andy. Andy, Eric says listen to me on my birthday. Over." He lets himself smile a little. Anyone who's listening on the emergency frequency is going to be confused. If only Andy is listening as well! Let's hope he understands the message. Eric stays on the emergency frequency for a while and then turns to 2110. Will Andy have understood his message and tuned in?

"Andy, do you hear me? Over," he whispers. He keeps on trying, but there is no answer.

Chapter 14. A stowaway aboard

THE FACT THAT Eric gets no response from Andy isn't surprising; the American is still unconscious. However, René isn't. He's as tough as nails and has been least affected by the drug. It's after midnight by the time he starts to come round. Pain pulses through his head like waves pounding a rocky coast. The first thing he's aware of is the smell of the carpet. Groaning, he opens an eye but struggles to focus. He remains lying on the floor in the dark, feeling sick with his head thumping. Where is he? What happened? Slowly memories start coming back to him: the fishing vessel, the grenades, the explosion. But where he is and how he got here, he can't remember. He opens an eye again, and using all his willpower, he lifts his head from the ground. It feels as if someone is turning a screwdriver in his brain, but ignoring the pain, he pulls himself up onto his side.

He can see in the dim moonlight that he's lying in the corridor. He must have tried to get inside, but he can't remember why. The last thing he remembers clearly is the fishing vessel approaching, and the grenade being launched. Did those guys come on board? What have they done?

He looks at his watch, but it's too dark to see, so he crawls to the door and opens it. The chilly night air does him some good, and he sits down outside with his back against the deckhouse and breathes in the fresh air. Slowly he starts to feel a bit better. As he gazes blankly across the deck, he becomes aware that something has changed. After a brief moment the truth suddenly dawns on him. The containers! The containers with the vaults are gone! Anger gives him the energy he needs to get up and confirm that the vaults are indeed gone. What's happened to the others? His eyes strain against the dark, and as he looks round he sees the outline of Mr Sterling lying near the electronic vault door. René goes over and checks his pulse. Sterling is still alive, but he's very cold. The Frenchman decides to put a blanket over him as he doesn't feel strong enough yet to carry him inside. Suddenly, he feels like a failure, a weakling. Mr Sterling had a lot of confidence in him believing that if something were to happen, René would jump into the breach. Sterling put a safe full of weapons at his disposal, and he wasn't even able to pick up a weapon never mind use one. He acted like a child and made a fool of himself. He sees professor de Wolff under the stairs and goes over to check on him. When he shakes his shoulder, the professor moans softly; he's starting to recover, but he's cold as well. Perhaps he should look for a bottle of cognac and bring it to the men.

Groaning at the heavy feeling in his head, he goes back inside. Everywhere he looks he finds unconscious expedition members. Most in bed. Some on the floor. Almost all of them are breathing heavily as if they are in a deep sleep. When he looks in the office — where the preservation and classification documents for the Titanic Treasures are kept — he sees that everything is gone; stolen. Where have they taken it all? Wait! Maybe their ship is still on the radar!

He quickly hurries to the radio room. Putting on the light, he sees Andy on the ground, still unconscious. René puts on the radar and the green light sweeps over the screen. Nothing! Too late! There is no sign of a boat. Where are the pirates heading? To Greenland? To Iceland? To America? They have no way of knowing.

He decides to go and see if he can help de Wolff who is likely to be the closest to coming to his senses. Maybe they can figure out something together. He may not always see eye to eye with de Wolff, but he's a guy you can rely on.

He goes back to the deck armed with a bottle of cognac from the bar. He gulps down a good portion himself first. The liquid burns his throat, and a pleasant warmth spreads to his stomach. He kneels down beside the professor whose eyes are already half open. They stare glassily at nothing.

"Hey, Willem, wake up!" René says as he gently shakes de Wolff's shoulder.

The professor turns his head and looks at him vacantly. Slowly his eyes start to focus as he returns to his senses. Luckily, he doesn't have a headache as bad as René's, but he feels stiff as a board from the long lie on the hard deck. A few sips of brandy do him some good though they bring tears to his eyes. René tells him what he's discovered. De Wolff's first thought is also to check the radar, but when he hears René has already done so, he fears the worst.

"We need to help the others first," he decides. "We can carry Sterling inside together. We can't leave him lying out on the deck."

After they have moved Sterling, they look to see who else they can help. Mr de Wolff checks on his own family next and puts Mrs de Wolff and Jessica in their beds. Bob is already in bed, but Mr de Wolff starts to feel anxious when he can't find Eric. He tells himself that Eric must just have been caught with the gas rifle in a quieter part of the boat, but as he continues to look, he starts to feel more and more worried. He can't find his son! By dawn, another two of the divers are awake, but nobody listens to the radio — the unit is not even switched on. Eric's call goes unheard, and his father's worry gives way to panic. Eric is still nowhere to be found, and nobody knows where he could be.

By the time Andy wakes up in the afternoon, there is still some confusion as to what exactly happened. The radio technician is one of the last to come round, and he decides to lay his cards on the table.

"It's all my fault," he begins and goes on to tell the whole story. At first, Sterling is furious, but as Andy explains what happened to his wife and child, he calms down a little, though not enough to be able to excuse Andy's betrayal.

"You deceived us from the very beginning," he says bitterly. "I took you on in good faith and paid you well, and you've broken my trust. You're a creep." René and most of the divers feel the same way; professor de Wolff is one of the few to stand by Andy.

"What was he supposed to do?" says the Dutch professor angrily.

"How do I know?" growls Sterling. "But I would never betray my comrades. It's an unwritten code."

"Have you any idea where Eric could be?" interrupts Mrs de Wolff desperately.

"I hid Eric in the radio room," says Andy. "Maybe he wasn't caught and saw what happened."

"Yes, but where is he now?" asks Bob. He's sitting next to Jessica and is one of the few who hasn't suffered in any way from a headache. Jessica hasn't had many unpleasant side effects either, but she remembers the attack by the guy in the mask, and it isn't doing her nerves any good at all.

"If he was hiding, he would have come out long ago," she says anxiously.

"They probably found him and threw him overboard", says René tactlessly. "Nobody wants a witness left to cause trouble."

Mrs de Wolff puts her hands to her mouth in horror, and the professor looks furiously at the huge Frenchman. That terrible thought has already been haunting him, but it hadn't yet occurred to Mrs de Wolff.

However, Eric is not in the sea. He's currently in the lifeboat fast asleep, and it's night before he wakes up again. He eats some of the emergency rations and waits until the crew have retreated and only the man on the bridge remains. Once he's certain the rest of the crew will be sleeping, he crawls out to stretch his legs and to relieve himself at the railing. Then he climbs as quietly as possible to the upper deck. From there he has a good view into the bridge, and if he strains his eyes, he can read the screen of the SATNAV. He memorises the coordinates on it.

He's back in the lifeboat half an hour later feeling a lot better. He pulls the radio towards him and finds the emergency frequency. He realises that, unlike last night, the man on the bridge will now be able to hear his message. But that's a risk he'll just have to take. With any luck, the man won't be able to make any sense of it.

"Eric to Andy. Andy, Eric says listen to me on my birthday. Over." He pulls the hood of the lifeboat back a little to check on the man on the bridge, but at this distance it's impossible to tell if he's listening or not.

"Eric calling Andy, Eric calling Andy, remember my birthday. Over."

He doesn't risk saying anything else but tunes in on frequency 2110 and transmits further from there. He doesn't get an answer.

"Hey, Andy! Wake up!"

Startled, Andy lifts his head from his pillows. He still has the remains of his headache and looks blankly at Dr Reynolds who is bending over him.

"What's up?" Andy says groggily.

"We got a message over the radio," the doctor replies. "Please come immediately!"

Andy rolls out of bed and follows the other man to the radio room. He sees at a glance that the radio is tuned to the emergency frequency.

"We heard the message on the bridge," the doctor explains, "and then we tuned in here."

"What's the message?" Andy wants to know, but before the doctor can answer, a voice comes from the radio.

"Eric calling Andy," it says. Andy's heart skips a beat. "It's Eric!" he whispers.

"Eric calling Andy! Think of my birthday! Come to my birthday!"

"Huh?" Andy mutters, the meaning of Eric's message not becoming immediately clear to him. He's not got over his astonishment at hearing Eric's voice over the radio. His thoughts tumble like acrobats. Eric's alive! Where is he? How did he get a radio? Birthday? Birthday? What does he mean by that?

At that moment, the door of the radio room flies open, and professor de Wolff and his wife burst in.

"A message from our Eric?" Mrs de Wolff asks, her voice breaking.

"Huh? Oh, yes, yes," stammers Andy. "He's calling me, talking about his birthday."

"Birthday?" the professor says, and suddenly Andy slaps his hand to his forehead.

"Of course!" he exclaims. "That's one bright kid! He knows that everyone can hear him on the emergency frequency, and he doesn't want to say anything more on it. I could be wrong, but I think he's on board the ship with the robbers."

"What?!" both the de Wolffs cry out, but Andy doesn't answer. He's too busy tuning the radio and looking for channel 2110. Then he waits in the hope that Eric will transmit at this frequency. Slowly the seconds tick by, and then, just as Andy is beginning to doubt whether he was right, he hears Eric's voice.

"Andy, can you hear me? Did you understand my message? Please answer."

"Yes!" cheers Andy, then immediately speaks into the microphone. "Hi Eric, I hear you loud and clear!"

Everyone can hear the boy's sigh of relief through the speaker.

"Finally!"

Mrs de Wolff also sighs audibly. She's been standing next to Mr de Wolff, but now she steps forward and grabs the microphone from Andy's hands.

"How does this thing work?" she says in a tone of voice that demands immediate answers.

"You can just talk," stammers Andy.

"Eric," says Mrs de Wolff, "you've no idea how relieved I am to hear you! Where are you? Are you ok?"

Eric is excited to hear his mother's voice, but it makes him realise how alone he's feeling. "I'm on board the boat with the robbers," he says, "hiding in a lifeboat. So far nobody's noticed me."

"Why did you get on board with them?!" asks his mother.

"Actually, I really don't know," Eric admits. "At the time it seemed a good idea to find out where they were going."

"Have you any idea where you are?" asks Mrs de Wolff.

"Yes," replies Eric. "I've just looked at their SATNAV."

"SATNAV?" says his mother.

"I know what he means," Andy says, his hand already reaching for the microphone. "Quickly, we don't know how long we'll be able to transmit for."

Mrs de Wolff returns the microphone to Andy, and Eric starts explaining everything that's happened. He tells Andy how the men with the gas rifles went on to transfer the treasures from the Titanic to another boat and how he stowed away on board.

"Their leader is called Mortimer," he says. "I've heard that name a few times."

"How did you get a radio?" Andy wants to know.

Andy becomes increasingly impressed as Eric tells him how he got the radio from the bridge.

"And you said you know where you are right now?" Andy enquires further.

"I learned the coordinates by heart," replies Eric.

"Wait," says Andy, "let me get the chart." He searches through the cupboards. "Ok, I'm ready."

Eric reels off the coordinates.

"Huh," says Andy surprised. "That's not what I was expecting to hear. Let me get a different chart, and in the meantime, you can talk to your parents." Andy beckons the professor over, and de Wolff takes his place behind the microphone. "You have no idea how glad I am to hear your voice, son!" he says.

Eric feels warm inside at the sound of his father's familiar voice. What he wouldn't give to be with him right now! "I'm scared, dad!" he says, very close to tears. "I never should have got on board this boat."

"We're looking at the chart to check where you are right now, son," says his father as reassuringly as possible, "and then we are on our way to get you."

Andy is looking with surprise at the chart. If he's been given the right coordinates, then the course of the boat makes no sense at all. He sits down behind the radio.

"Eric," he begins, "you're on the way to Hudson Bay. Why they're heading there, I don't know; it's a completely deserted area, but we're coming, so don't worry. Don't transmit anymore on the emergency frequency! I'll leave the radio open at 2110, and if you find out anything else, you can let us know."

They talk for a moment longer and then disconnect. Eric peers through a crack in the hood, and to his horror, he sees Mortimer walking on the bridge. Did they hear? Surely that's impossible; the whole conversation took place on frequency 2110. Eric reassures himself that there's no way they could have heard from the bridge, but he can't shake the uneasy feeling.

"Why did you wake me up?" Mortimer demands grumpily. Jerry doesn't know how to begin. Yesterday he was in charge of the raid on the Aquatic Dream, and now he must admit he's made mistakes.

"I had the radio on the emergency frequency," he begins, "and I heard a strange message that was crystal clear, as if it were transmitted very closely."

"Hmm," grumbles Mortimer, not yet interested.

"The message said 'Eric to Andy. Think of my birthday'," Jerry explains further.

"Did you wake me up just for that?" Mortimer asks angrily. "Some fool who abused the distress signal?"

"The radio technician on the Aquatic Dream is called Andy," Jerry replies.

"So what?" retorts Mortimer.

"Yesterday, after we secured the boat, we checked the list to make sure everyone was down and out," Jerry begins.

Mortimers eyes sparkle. "You said that everyone was unconscious."

"That's right," Jerry says anxiously, "but there was one person we couldn't find, one of the sons of the Dutch professor, and because it was just a kid, we didn't follow it up any further."

"And what's that got to do with the radio message?"

"The boy is called Eric, sir!"

Mortimer needs no further explanations. "You think he's climbed on board here," he muses aloud, "but how is he sending messages?" Suddenly, he swears loudly, and turning around, he throws open the cupboard door hiding the emergency radio. Empty!

"That kid is definitely on board!" he yells. "He's stolen the radio, and he's keeping the others informed about where we're going."

Pieces of the puzzle are falling into place — the "accident" with the helmsman yesterday when the kid obviously took the radio. Mortimer bites his lip. He has to admit that was a clever stunt.

"Where will he be hiding?" Jerry asks.

Mortimer looks out over the deck which is shrouded in darkness. He can just make out the contours of the lifeboats.

"He'll be in one of those boats," is his confident opinion.

"Shall we grab him?" Jerry asks eagerly.

"There's no rush," Mortimer says thoughtfully. "Sterling likes to play chess, and he thinks he's one step ahead of me now. Maybe I can take advantage of this situation. If he comes after me into the wilderness, it's just him against me. It's a game with high stakes, and I think I'm going to play along. Let the kid sit tight for the moment. Make him think he's safe. This trip may end up providing me with more than the vaults of the Titanic. Maybe much more."

A sly smile spreads across his lips.

Chapter 15. An abandoned mine in Ungava Bay

THE FOLLOWING NIGHT Eric switches the radio on again and makes contact with Andy. Last night was a long night though it was a relief to speak with his parents. Andy instructed him to creep back to the top deck — where he could see into the bridge — and to try and find out what sort of radar Mortimer's boat has. He did as he was asked and reported back in detail. Andy recognised the model. He said that it didn't have as wide a range as the one on the Aquatic Dream which meant the Aquatic Dream would be able to get close without anyone aboard the Rubicon realising that they were being followed.

Eric didn't allow himself to use the radio the following day. The foredeck was in regular use, and there was too great a risk that he would be heard. He was relieved when night came again and he could establish contact.

"Are you there, Andy?" asks Eric.

"Yes, boy!" replies the American, and Eric can hear the smile in his voice. "I have good news for you: we have you on radar!"

"What?!" whispers Eric, elated. "You know exactly where I am?"

"Practically to the yard kiddo," says Andy as reassuringly as possible.

"What a relief!" sighs Eric. For a moment he feels safe, and then Andy's tone becomes more serious.

"You have to stay hidden now," he says, "don't take risks and go out of your hiding place unnecessarily. Sterling got his private detectives to investigate who Mortimer is, and the information has just come back to us. He is definitely not somebody that you want to mess with. You've got yourself on board a ship with some of the worst criminals in the United States. If you enter a port, and there's a chance to escape, then you should get the hell out."

This speech terrifies Eric. He witnessed the robbery and was aware that he was among crooks, but he didn't realise they were quite so dangerous.

"Will they kill me if they find me?" he whispers into the microphone. Andy knows that this is not impossible, but he doesn't say so to Eric.

"Well, it won't come to that, but don't take risks! If you get an opportunity to get away from them, then take it."

"Okay," Eric replies in a small voice.

"Hang on in there, boy," the radio technician reassures him, "here's your father for a minute."

While Eric talks with his father, the Rubicon makes its way into Ungava Bay. The Aquatic Dream is still at the top of the Button islands, and Sterling stands on the bridge looking at the dot on the radar.

"Ungava Bay," he mutters, "what do they want there? It's almost nothing but wilderness, just a couple of tiny harbours, and a small fishing community."

"I can't imagine they'll take the vaults ashore there," the captain agrees, "it really is the middle of nowhere."

The Rubicon powers purposefully along the east coast of the bay. Despite the late hour, Mortimer is still awake. He has been staying awake as much as possible to manage the developments of the last couple of days.

"What time will we arrive?" he asks the helmsman.

The man looks at the SATNAV, then on the map, and finally at his watch.

"Tonight at seven," he says shortly.

"Do you see Sterling's boat on the radar yet?" Mortimer wants to know.

The helmsman shakes his head.

"That's to be expected," Mortimer smiles. "He has a more powerful radar then we do, and he'll want to stay out of our range, but I bet he's following."

"Aren't you afraid he'll call the police?" asks the helmsman, a little worried.

Mortimer shakes his head. "Sterling is a man who has become successful by always taking care of his own interests. He likes to stay in control. In this game, he'll be thinking in terms of move and countermove; he'll want to outmanoeuvre me by himself."

"And you're not afraid he'll manage it?" asks the helmsman.

Mortimer smiles frostily. "I also like chess. Sterling thinks he's one step ahead of us because the kid's on board; he thinks he's going to surprise me. He doesn't realise I already know about the kid which puts me one step ahead of him. I know how he thinks. No, he won't go to the police; he'll come himself, but he's no idea what he's getting himself into."

"What are you actually planning?" says professor de Wolff to Sterling angrily. Mrs de Wolff, Andy, and René are in the radio room. The sun has just risen, but aboard the Aquatic Dream everyone has been up for hours. They're still pursuing the Rubicon, but the professor wants to know what Sterling imagines is going to happen once they catch up.

"Simple!" replies the billionaire. "Thanks to your son we know exactly where Mortimer is going. Once his boat docks in a harbour, we'll turn off our radar, spy on them for some more information, and take whatever opportunity presents itself for getting the Titanic treasures back again."

"Have you never heard of the police or the army?" exclaims Mrs de Wolff, as angry as her husband. "You're surely not planning to take on those guys alone! You'll put all of our lives at risk."

"That's exactly what I'm planning," Sterling jumps in, no less passionately. "I have modern weapons on board. I have a crew and a dive team who are well trained, and your husband doesn't come across as a pushover either."

"I am not," says de Wolff," and I demand that you contact the police! Two of my children are on this boat, and my other son is in immediate danger. We need help."

"Now think for a minute, man!" says the billionaire. "If we call the police, the whole world will find out that the vaults have been lifted, and the international press will be all over us. When it comes out that the vaults fell into the hands of criminals, all those who wanted the Titanic left in peace will have the story they need to create endless waves of bad publicity. If we get them back, and then involve the press, it will be like a giant publicity stunt. I can see the headlines already: "Titanic's vaults safely back after dramatic chase." The success of the exhibition will be guaranteed; it'll be sold out round the world."

"Is that all you care about?" booms the professor. "The money?! I'm thinking of my children and everyone else aboard this boat. Well, if the Titanic treasures are so valuable to you, why put them at risk? If there's a showdown, they'll be in danger of being irreversibly damaged."

"Danger?" laughs Sterling scornfully. "All we need is a simple plan and some follow up action. Nothing's going to go wrong. We're a step ahead of Mortimer, and we need to use it to our advantage. Anyway, we're at the edge of the world. Where are you going to find your policemen?"

"Even this island can be reached by helicopter," argues the professor, "but we need to contact them now to give them time to get here. I'm sure your company would be able to get help through its contacts too. Sterling is a world renowned name."

The billionaire shakes his head. "I'm in charge," he says stubbornly. "It happens my way, and that's it!"

"There is no way 'that's it'!" bursts out Mrs de Wolff. She turns to Andy, "Andy, you make contact with Montréal or Québec right away and see who is best positioned to help out." Andy hesitates. He's inclined to agree with the de Wolffs, but he's still weighing up everything that's been said.

"Andy is doing nothing," roars Sterling. "It was Andy that put us all in this mess. He'll do exactly what I say now. If I'd had it my way, I'd have put him off this boat long ago."

"You think this is my fault? My fault?!" Andy snaps. "I've wanted to involve the police from the start, and I'm going to do it right now." He sits down at the radio and puts the headphones on.

"What?!" roars Sterling. "René, stop him!"

The French giant steps forwards but the professor moves between him and the radio technician.

"You want to fight over the radio?" he says menacingly.

Sterling has had enough. From under his jacket he pulls out a gun, and the professor and Andy freeze when the weapon swings in their direction. Sterling pulls the trigger three times. The bullets penetrate deep into the bowels of the radio, and the device breaks down with a bang.

"So," says the billionaire, "end of discussion."

De Wolff flies over and grabs the billionaire by the lapels of his jacket.

"I've studied the history of the Titanic," he spits. "The rich people were the first in the lifeboats. They were saved. The rest of the passengers were trapped behind barriers that were only opened at the last minute. Nearly all of them drowned. I thought something had changed since then, but you still think that just because you have money you're better than everybody else and should be able to do whatever you want." He shoves the American away from him in disgust.

Sterling regains his balance, dusts off his lapels, and says nothing. He walks out the radio room inwardly seething and heads up the steps to the bridge. Ripping open the box containing the emergency radio, he grabs the device, heads out on deck, and flings it overboard into the waves of Ungava Bay.

"What are you doing?" asks the startled captain in surprise.

"Mind your own business," snarls Sterling.

The captain shuts his mouth when he sees the look in the eyes of the tycoon.

The de Wolffs head to their cabin. The professor sits down on the edge of his bed and stares in front of him with unseeing eyes. Mrs de Wolff sits down next to him and puts her hand on his shoulder.

"You're thinking of Eric, aren't you?" she whispers.

De Wolff nods. "I'm sorry, Elise!" he says.

"Sorry about what?" his wife says.

"I didn't have to go on this expedition," says the professor.

"You didn't sign up for this," says his wife.

De Wolff shakes his head. "I let myself get carried along by the emotion of it all. A trip to the Titanic — it sounded like a fairytale — but when you read more about what happened when it was sinking, it is disturbing. The people without money were trapped behind barriers; they didn't stand a chance. Yet the first class women and children were helped into the lifeboats. Most of the lifeboats had been removed before the ship even sailed so the rich had more walking space.

At first, I just thought the ship itself was interesting, but I've been increasingly thinking about the different groups of people. What must have gone through the minds of those left behind, when one after another the lifeboats left with the rich, and all that remained was the certainty of death on the icy sea? It's ironic that now we find our own lives put at risk by the decisions of a wealthy man protecting his own interests."

"We've been given a lifeboat," says Elise de Wolff, softly.

The professor turns to her not immediately understanding what she means, but when he sees her serious eyes he knows whom she's referring to. He smiles.

"You're right," he says, "and on that lifeboat it doesn't matter how thick your wallet is."

"Willem, you call on Him if you feel you've done something stupid!"

"Let's do that, Elise!"

Eric strains to try and see through a gap in the lifeboat cover. He's really not sure what to do. He's been trying all day to make contact with Andy, but for some obscure reason, the 2110 frequency produces only white noise. What's happened? Have they given up the chase? They wouldn't abandon him, would they? His parents would never give up looking for him. He's confident of that, but for the moment it seems he is alone again. He could really use some advice at this moment. He looks out again as the sun sinks into the horizon and turns the water red. It seems they might be nearing their final destination as they are travelling close to land now, only about one hundred yards out from shore. Sloping hills stretch along the water, and the terrain is rocky. All day they've been powering past this majestic landscape, but it just makes Eric feel desolate inside; little vegetation; no houses; no people; nothing. Andy explained yesterday that they were in the north of Canada, somewhere in the inhospitable region of Labrador. It certainly seems inhospitable.

He's wondered a few times what Mortimer is doing here, and as they approach a little harbour, it seems he has the answer to his question. With the last of the daylight starting to fade, Eric can just about make out where they are headed. Some abandoned piers along a natural bay have produced a simple port. He can see that beyond the port there is a village made up of identical prefabricated houses. In between the port and the houses are large barns. The village is surrounded by high hills that look like giant wigwams. Eric suddenly remembers a chapter of his geography book and realises what they are. Piles of mining waste. So the huge building built on the hillside over there must be a mine. Where there's a mine, there are people, and people have phones! Maybe he can call for help from there.

Mortimer's boat powers right on into the harbour, and Eric wonders why Mortimer is not concerned about people seeing the vaults. They're still lying in their containers on the open deck where anybody could see them. Won't people be curious? Eric thinks about what to do next and taps his fingers on his chin indecisively.

With his hands behind his back, Mortimer gazes out in satisfaction from the bridge of the Rubicon as they approach the port. "Almost home, boys!" he says to the helmsman and skipper with undisguised pleasure. "We'll plan out our work when we arrive. These vaults have to be opened, and we need to see exactly what's in the crates. Then we need to look at setting up a distribution network."

"That lot will bring in a pretty penny," says the helmsman.

"This little island visit will yield even more," says Mortimer giving a sudden bright smile. "Sterling is on his way, and once he arrives, he won't escape easily. I'll make sure I bleed him dry; the Sterling empire will be mine. Imagine! Legal connections to virtually every US industry; we'll be able to launder billions of dollars; we'll have power that even Al Capone didn't dare dream of!"

"What should we do with the little guy?" asks the captain. "He'll have seen by now that we've reached a port."

Mortimer nods. "You're right, the lad must not escape. A hostage might prove to be worth his weight in gold. We'll get someone to catch him while we're still at sea. Ten to one he's in the front lifeboat."

The captain uses the intercom to call Jerry to the bridge.

"You can grab the kid now," orders Mortimer. "Lock him up in a cabin, and make sure there's no way he can get out."

Jerry nods. He's wearing a shoulder holster over his commando sweater, and he pulls out a heavy revolver and leaves the bridge. With a shrill whistle he attracts the attention of another guy who comes over.

"Mortimer wants us to nab our guest," says Jerry, and the other man — who already knows about the stowaway — also takes a large revolver from his shoulder holster.

Jerry signals to the bridge, and the captain puts on the bow lights. With the deck suddenly bathed in light, the lifeboat stands out brightly against the now almost black sky. The gangsters approach the lifeboat from opposite sides, and Jerry grabs the edge of the cover. With both guns pointing to the lifeboat, he throws up the tarpaulin.

"Freeze!"

There's no boy to frighten inside the lifeboat. Jerry's eyes wander over the pillows lying on the floor, the food wrappers, and the stolen radio, but there is no trace of Eric himself. Jerry yells some impressive expletives out to sea. Where did the brat go?!

The skipper of the Aquatic Dream looks intently at the radar, and Sterling watches over his shoulder. The billionaire has barely left the bridge; he wants to monitor the chase minute by minute.

"I think they've reached their destination," says the captain, "their speed has reduced, and they're coming closer to shore."

Sterling trusts the experienced sailor's conclusion and pulls out a map. Where is their destination? The map shows nothing, nowhere of interest where they might go ashore. Sterling searches angrily in the cabinet for a more detailed map. He can't find one, but he does come across an older map that for some reason has never been cleared out. Without much hope, Sterling opens the ten year old map and scans the shoreline.

"Hey," he says, suddenly surprised, and leans in closer, "there does seem to be something on this map."

The captain comes over. "Labrador Mining Trust," he reads aloud.

"A mine?" Sterling asks.

"There are more of them here," says the captain. "The hills in these places can be rich in minerals. They drill in a few shafts, put a building up against them, throw up a few prefab houses round about, and within a few months a mining town is born.

"Hmm," growls Sterling, "then why is it no longer on the map? A town doesn't just disappear into nothing?"

"Sometimes they do," the captain replies enigmatically.

Eric has never felt so miserable in his whole life. For a moment he doubts that he will make it. He allows his freezing arms to rest for a moment and floats in the water of the bay looking back at the boat. He's about halfway to the shore now. It seemed so simple: jump overboard, swim to shore, find someone with a radio or phone, and call for help. From the moment he climbed over the railing and dropped into the water, he realised it wasn't going to be easy. For starters, the cold of the water was paralyzing, and as the hull of the Rubicon slid past him like a dark wall, he saw the powerful propellers heading towards him. He began swimming desperately to avoid being sucked in, but the water began to swirl and fizz around him, and he felt himself being pulled down. Every second he expected the searing pain of an arm or a leg coming into contact with the propeller. Slowly, the water became calmer, and when he finally surfaced spluttering, the Rubicon was past him. Then he began the swim to shore. Eric considered himself a good swimmer, and at a glance it didn't seem too far, but swimming in a pool or natural pond at home, in the Netherlands, was different to this. In Egypt, he often swam in the river, but the cool water was always pleasant after the sweltering heat. There was nothing pleasurable about this. The water was his enemy. A mortal enemy.

Now he struggles to escape its grasp, and the cold cuts into him. The shore isn't too far away, but the distance seems endless. Eric looks back at the Rubicon and is surprised to see light suddenly flashing onto the front deck. Two guys sneak up to the lifeboat where he was hiding just a few minutes ago. He sees them pull back the cover. Wow! That was a narrow escape.

Suddenly it dawns on him that this is actually very strange. He wasn't discovered all the time they were at sea, and now that they are approaching a port, these guys seem to know exactly where he was hiding. How can that be? A suspicion is growing. Could they have known all along where he was? If so, why didn't they discover him? He doesn't understand, but he can't think about it now; he clenches his teeth and swims on. The cold is so intense that it seems simpler just to give up and let himself sink to the icy depths. Fighting against this temptation, he concentrates on swimming a stroke, two strokes, three, ten, and then starting again. The shore is getting closer, but slowly, much too slowly.

The Rubicon has now reached the port, and there are men standing ready on the quay. There are about a dozen in the usual dark commando sweaters. One of them flicks a cigarette butt into the water, and then they spread out along the jetty ready to catch the mooring ropes as they are thrown.

A few minutes later, the gangway is coming down, and Mortimer is one of the first off the boat. There is a buggy at the end of the jetty, and he climbs in and drives off through the streets in the direction of the largest building. The village has a bleak appearance like a modern version of a western ghost town. The buggy moves easily along the bumpy path until it reaches the main building of the mine. It looks deserted from the outside. The doors are rusty, the windows dirty, and most of the diamond shaped window panes have disappeared. Mortimer grabs a small remote control hanging by a rubber strap next to the steering wheel and presses a button. The heavy, rusty doors glide open noiselessly, and from within the seemingly abandoned building spills out a very modern looking sea of bright light. The buggy rides into a substantial hall — brightly lit by striplights in long lines along the ceiling — filled with a number of trucks with large tyres. The mine may look deserted from the outside, but inside is a different story.

Eric has only a few more yards to go, but it feels like a mile. His arms are hardly moving, and he's swimming on autopilot now, although in his head he's still counting the strokes. Then suddenly, his trainers touch a stone on the bottom and with a few stumbling steps over the rocks, he is out of the water. The balmy, evening breeze blows around him. The commando sweater, which he dared not get rid of, is hanging to his knees. Small streams of water run down it and flow through his jeans to the ground. Eric's teeth are chattering with the cold; he may be out the water, but if he doesn't find warm shelter soon, his swim will kill him yet. He pulls the sweater off and wrings as much water out of it as possible, and then he does the same with his shirt and trousers. He feels slightly more comfortable putting them on again but still cold. He needs to get to that village quickly. Trying to get his bearings, he concludes that it should be somewhere behind the hill lying in front of him. He finds a narrow goat path that takes him to the top, and sure enough, he can see the vague outline of the village below. Strange, there are no lights. Why is that? He doesn't have time to think about it and hurries down the slope, desperate for warmth. Finding a path that is more weeds than paving stones, he reaches the first house and bangs on the door with his fist. There is no noise from inside. He thumps on the door again. He doesn't dare to shout as he is now not far from the harbour. Still no sign of life. He grabs the door handle, and not only does he find that the door is not locked, but the hinges are so corroded that at the slightest pressure the handle slides out of Eric's fingers, and with a thud, the door falls flat in the hallway. Eric keeps his balance with difficulty.

"Now that's what I call dropping in," he mumbles to no one.

The house is empty, and it looks like it's been that way for some time. As he walks back out, the truth hits him; nobody lives here anymore. The big building sitting against the mountain was probably some kind of factory that has now closed; the workers long gone. He shudders in the cold light of the fully shining moon. A deserted village! What should he do? What is Mortimer doing here anyway? The gangster is definitely here; he could see the boat when he was at the top of the hill. He's tempted to walk back to it and hide in the lifeboat again, but that place is no longer safe, and he's not going to get warm enough there anyway. It all seemed so simple: find a phone and the job would be done; but there are no active phone lines in this village. He can only hope the Aquatic Dream is still on her way, but even this hope is dwindling. Why did they stop answering the radio?

He's really not sure where to go but decides to head towards the old factory. Finding the road isn't difficult — the huge building rises above everything. The only thing higher is something in the village that looks like a tower built of steel beams. He runs between two deserted houses and then stops suddenly. Next to the factory is a large empty piece of ground, and on a strip of concrete — standing out against the night sky — are the silhouettes of two huge transport helicopters. If they didn't have the moonlit sky as a backdrop, he probably wouldn't have seen them standing there in the dark. They are covered with camouflage nets to make them invisible from the air. Eric runs towards them. The nets are held up by poles, forming a sort of huge tent covering the giants of the air. When the boy gets closer, he sees that the helicopters are not old and rusted but well cared for machines. He hoists himself up the steps of one of them so he can look inside. Soft green lights illuminate a modern dashboard display.

Eric is getting more and more confused. What are these things doing here? He jumps back onto the ground which he notes is covered with well-maintained concrete slabs. He's becoming warmer from all the movement. His teeth still chatter, and despite having eaten before jumping into the water, he wouldn't say no to another meal. He'd preferably have something hot, but there's no point in thinking about it. He resumes his journey to the factory, and as he gets closer, he can hear a low growl. Almost automatically, he turns towards the large rolling shutters, but the sound seems to be coming from elsewhere: a low building that's been built up against the factory. Eric decides to take a look. Carefully — to avoid a sudden confrontation with Mortimer's men — he sneaks over to it. Once there, he decides the sound is produced by several machines humming. His hand closes around the handle, and he carefully pushes the door open a little. A pleasant warmth comes from inside. Eric tries to look around, but he can't see much. The warmth is too much of a temptation, and he quickly slips inside. The heat is like a blanket around him. It would probably be uncomfortably hot in here normally, but Eric loves it. He stands with his eyes closed for a moment, and then he looks around. A weak light illuminates the room, and he can see large boilers with all kinds of meters and pipes. In fact, there are pipes of all different sizes as far as the eye can see. Eric holds out his hand towards one which is as thick as a tree trunk. Even from a distance he can feel that the pipe is warm. He quickly pulls off his commando sweater and hangs it over the pipe. He turns it after a few minutes and steam comes up from the sweater as if it were being freshly ironed. Apparently, this is some kind of boiler room piping heat into the factory which obviously isn't abandoned; Mortimer is using it. What he's using it for, Eric can only guess. He wishes his parents were here, and Bob, and Jessica too. He's missing them terribly.

Chapter 16. A new confrontation

"HOW FAR IN will I go, Mr Sterling?" asks the helmsman. The billionaire looks at the radar. They are only a few miles from the harbour, it should be just behind that stretch of cape.

"We'll drop anchor here next to the shore," Sterling decides.

Everyone is on the bridge, and the tension is palpable. De Wolff is still the spokesman for those who don't want to fight, and this group includes Mr and Mrs de Wolff and their children, Andy, and professor Magnussen. They are suggesting that instead, they make every effort to get outside help, but they are easily outnumbered by those who side with Sterling.

The only two who have not joined the debate are Mrs Sterling and Dr Reynolds. Goldie has seemed lost since her pleasure trip of spending and sightseeing took a darker turn. She just sits apathetically on a chair and says nothing. Doctor Reynolds is struggling to make up his mind. In his heart he agrees with de Wolff, but as a doctor he feels compelled to go with Sterling. His help could prove to be desperately needed if there was a battle.

The others are one hundred percent behind Sterling. Some want to shoot live ammunition, but the billionaire has vetoed this suggestion saying that if it ends in a bloodbath, it will lead to bad publicity. No, tranquilliser darts should be used. They should be stalking them, taking Mortimer's men out one at a time, then imprisoning them and contacting the police or the army. The men nod. Great! Good plan!

De Wolff wants to say something, but he realises it's like talking to a brick wall. The men from the diving team consider him a softy that wants others to do his dirty work for him and will barely look at him. This hurts the professor because he is not at all afraid, at least not for himself. However, he is scared for his son who is going to be caught in the crossfire between the two groups. He holds his tongue as the seeds of an alternative plan start to grow in his mind.

The Aquatic Dream's anchor has been let down, and she lies still while the 'battle group' leave the bridge. They open the weapons room and arm themselves generously before lowering the lifeboats and climbing in. Two boats full of guys armed to the teeth. As they start the engines, de Wolff puts his hand on Andy's shoulder.

"You are a miracle worker with radios," he says quietly. "Do you think you can get the wrecked radio up and running?"

Andy smiles mysteriously, pleased with the confidence placed in him.

"I opened the device up yesterday," he says, "and I think I can repair it, pretty easily actually, but the unit needs to be taken apart. I didn't dare do it yesterday in case Sterling caught me and completely destroyed it. I did as much as I could without taking it apart to save us time today. If I start now, I reckon I could have it up and running in about half an hour.

"Do it now!" the professor urges.

Bob and Jessica look at each other. If they had the radio, they might be able to contact Eric again, but Mr de Wolff has other plans. They need police backup, or rather the military, but he needs to be able to convince them that their story is true.

The lifeboats speed along the coast, and Sterling points to a rocky outcrop on the shore. If they head over there, they should be able to climb the rocks and get a good view of the mine and village on the other side. The moon casts an eerie light; ideal weather for their plans.

"We'll go ashore here!" he commands. "I'll head up those rocks with some men, and we'll come and report back."

What he can't see in the dark is the two men in commando sweaters sitting on those very rocks. They watch the approaching boats through their night vision goggles.

"Time to signal Mr Mortimer," says one of them. The other man pulls a mobile from his pocket and taps in a number.

"Mr Mortimer, Sterling is on his way to Barclay Rock. We can see two lifeboats heading straight for us.

"Fine!" says Mortimer. "Make yourselves scarce for the moment! He'll want to see the mine. Let him come up, but call me again if he goes back to board his boat."

"Yes, sir!"

Sterling's boat is the first to reach the small rocky beach at the foot of Barclay Rocks. He beckons to René to go with him, and together they clamber up the gentle slope. From there the moonlight allows them a reasonable view of the mining complex, but the helicopters are not visible from this angle.

"Seems deserted," says René.

"The vaults are still on the boat," Sterling notes. "If we can board the boat and take its crew out, we're good. We could snatch Mortimer's boat from right under his nose."

René agrees with him. "We could motor the boats round the cape and then row the last part to make sure there's no noise. Then we tie up the lifeboats at the jetty near the Rubicon. The gangway is still down; it's not going to be a problem to get on board."

Sterling nods. "We'll do that," he says.

The de Wolff family and professor Magnusson watch anxiously as Andy tinkers with the radio.

"Is it working?" Bob asks impatiently. He's been full of frustrated energy the last few days because there's been nothing he can do to help Eric. Deep down he wanted to go with the men in the lifeboats, but he was wise enough to keep his mouth shut. Now he bounces excitedly on the balls of his feet.

"Quiet, quiet!" grumbles Andy as he turns the screws in a cable connector. "If it's going to work, we should see something now," he says, more to himself than to the others. He cautiously flicks a switch, and white noise comes from the speakers.

"Yes!" says Andy elated. "Well, boys, there you have it!"

"What are you going to do now?" Magnussen wants to know.

"The nearest town of any size is a place with the beautiful name of Hebron," Andy explains while he keeps working on the radio. "There should be a police station there. Let's just hope they'll believe us."

"Why wouldn't they believe us?" Bob asks.

"Well," says Andy, "if I were a cop and I got someone on the line telling me the vaults of the Titanic have just been taken to a deserted bay by a gang of crooks, and the person calling wants help getting them back, I'm not sure I'd believe them."

"Goodness," said Bob, "I hadn't thought of that."

"I've thought about it a lot," says Andy grimly.

Sergeant Norris, head of the police station in Hebron, lifts his feet off the table as one of his subordinates puts his head round the door.

"What d'ya want?" growls the policeman, who is not known for his friendly manner.

"There's a guy on the radio," says the man.

"Elton John or Mick Jagger?" Norris says, being deliberately difficult.

"No, sir, this looks serious. This man claims he's the radio technician from a Titanic Expedition. He's calling us from Ungava Bay."

"If they're looking for the Titanic there, they'll be looking awhile," grumbles Norris. "Must be a prank call," he crossly pulls his two hundred pounds body out of the chair and walks through to the adjoining room where the radio is.

"Sergeant Norris, Hebron police," blasts his voice as he pulls the microphone towards him. "So you can't find the Titanic?"

When he hears the unfriendly tone of the policeman, Andy realises how this conversation is likely to go and purses his lips in frustration. De Wolff lays a hand on his shoulder.

"Let me," Willem says. Andy moves over, and the professor takes his place behind the microphone. He introduces himself and explains in his best English what's going on. Norris doesn't interrupt him once, and the professor only occasionally hears a grunt as if Norris has understood something. When he's finished speaking, Norris finally responds.

"So, if I understand correctly, your leader, who is called Sterling, has gone in by himself?"

"Yes," replies the professor.

"That's hard to believe," says Norris. "Anyone with half a brain in his head would have involved the police a long time ago."

"You don't know Sterling," replies the professor, "he's used to solving his own problems. That's why he's become one of the richest men in the world."

"It's not a very convincing story," Norris coolly observes.

"What? Not convincing!?" the professor says angrily. "The life of my son and a lot of other people is at stake here. If something happens to them because of your negligence, I'll hold you personally responsible! I hope that sounds convincing enough! Contact the Sterling group! If they hear what's happened, they'll take whatever steps necessary to protect their company and its director."

Norris looks over his shoulder to where two other agents are listening with interest. "What do you make of this?" he sighs, shaking his head.

Sterling has come down from the rocks, and the two men remain watching in the darkness. One stands with his foot against a rock, and when he sees the two boats heading round the cape, he pulls his mobile out again.

"Mr Mortimer, Sterling has gone back to his boat, and they're heading in your direction."

"Fine," comes Mortimer's voice over the phone.

"Gentlemen, the game is about to begin!" Mortimer says to a group of his men in his office deep in the mine. "You know what to do." The guys nod and quickly move out of the office.

Eric is still in the boiler room. His clothes are dry and warm from the pipes, and he is having to work hard not to fall asleep. Hurried footsteps from outside rouse him from his languor, and he feels a burst of adrenalin shoot through him. There is more than one person running about, something's going on out there. Something to worry about? He wonders about hiding, but decides instead to try and find out what's going on and cautiously opens the door a crack. He can hear activity in the distance, but there's nobody to be seen around the boiler room. Seeing some bushes he could hide in for a better view, he slips out of the door, runs across, and dives down under them. Now he can see what's going on: a couple of men are pulling the camouflage nets from the helicopters, and others with helmets, presumably the pilots, are climbing into the cockpits. Moments later, the rear doors of the heavy transport helicopters are lowered, and a dozen or so men carrying guns run into each. Fear wraps around Eric like a blanket. He has no doubt those guys are going to attack the boat his family is on. What can he do? He can't think of anything and can only watch as the engines roar and the enormous blades begin to rotate. Eric can feel the earth trembling and a cold wind blasting towards him, and moments later, the two giants lift from the ground and head towards their prey.

Sterling looks stunned when the big helicopters suddenly fly out of the darkness towards them. Hanging from their bellies are bright searchlights, and there is no time for Sterling and his party to escape. The lights glide systematically over the dark water until one is inevitably turned on them, and they are first dazzled, then blinded, as the other lights turn their way. René is the first to respond. He takes his weapon out and directs it upwards before remembering it's only loaded with tranquilliser darts. He shoots anyway in the direction of the spotlights; maybe he can smash them, and they might escape under the protection of darkness, but the darts do about as much damage as a toy gun would do to an elephant.

The response of the men in the helicopters is instant. Several machine gun rounds are fired into the water around Sterling's boat. Fortunately for those in the lifeboats, Mortimer has given orders to capture everyone alive. A loudspeaker hangs from the bottom of one of the helicopters, and the commanding voice of the pilot booms out from it. The message is short and to the point; they are to throw their weapons overboard and sit down with their hands on their heads.

René is shaking with fury at the nightmare situation, never in his life has he been so easily fooled. Sterling realises that the game, at least for now, is over. He angrily throws his gun into the sea, and the others follow his example. With hands on their heads, they wait for the next move. A side door of the helicopter slides open, ropes roll down, and soon some heavily armed men are on their way down. Jumping into the lifeboats, they take over the controls and hold the crew at gunpoint.

A few minutes later, the two boats are on their way to the port where the Rubicon is moored; one of the transport helicopters flies above them lighting the scene.

Those aboard the Aquatic Dream are unaware of the fate of Sterling's group. De Wolff is still doing his best to convince Norris that he is telling the truth, but he's having little success.

"What can I say to convince you?" the professor asks angrily.

"Well, come up with another story," Norris replies cynically.

At this point Bob, who is closest to the door, hears something and goes to take a look outside. To his horror, he sees a helicopter silhouetted against the sky like a giant insect, coming in their direction. Jessica sees it as well.

"There's a helicopter coming!" she shouts frantically.

"A helicopter?" asks professor Magnussen, shocked. "That can only be Mortimer." De Wolff reaches the same conclusion. A moment later the helicopter is hanging over them and its roar resonates throughout the boat.

"Do you hear that?" de Wolff yells into the microphone. "That's a helicopter, we're being attacked!" He looks through the windows where spotlights light up the whole deck and sees men with machine guns sliding down from the helicopter on ropes. Once on the deck, they fan out, weapons at the ready. De Wolff describes everything he's seeing to Norris.

"You must take immediate action!" he says urgently.

Norris doesn't answer.

Two men are already running across the deck and into the radio room.

"Everyone on the floor, hands on your head!" shouts the first man who gets inside.

Jessica sinks down immediately. Magnussen is already on his knees from sheer fright. Bob looks at his mother. She is standing with her hands by her side looking in confusion at the intruder as if she doesn't understand what he's saying.

"Wat moeten jullie hier?" 'What are you doing here?' she says in Dutch.

The second man arrives behind the first, and for a moment, they are nonplussed by the lack of cooperation from Mrs de Wolff.

"On the ground!" barks the second guy and gives Bob a rough push in the back. Bob kneels down, and the man with the gun gestures for his mother to do the same, but Bob sees her squaring her shoulders defiantly. What's she playing at?!

"Mum, look out!" he screams, seeing that the guy is starting to become angry.

"Are you still listening?" says professor de Wolff into the microphone. He too remains standing, and Bob suddenly understands why his mother is putting on a show of not understanding: she is buying more time for the police to hear what's going on. One of the intruders reaches the same conclusion and aims his weapon at the radio. De Wolff has just enough time to dive aside before the speeding bullet blows the radio to smithereens.

"Anything from the man in Hebron?" says Mrs de Wolff to her husband softly a few moments later. He's lying beside her on the ground with his arm around her.

"No," replies the professor. "I'm not even sure he was still listening."

Meanwhile, Mortimer's team have come together to discuss their next move. They force the prisoners out onto the deck where the transport helicopter hovers just a few feet up. The pilot really knows how to handle the machine. The de Wolff family, Andy, Mrs Sterling and professor Magnusson are directed to climb into the back. The blast from the giant rotor blades almost blows them off their feet, but Mortimer's men grab them by the shoulders and push them into the belly of the machine. The door closes, and looking at the grim faces of the robbers, Jessica feels a level of fear she's never known before.

The helicopter rises above the Aquatic Dream, and they are on their way to Mortimer's base — right into the lion's den.

Chapter 17. The game of death or dollars

THE BRIGHT LIGHTS on the ceiling in Mortimer's base illuminate a curious scene. Professor de Wolff is tied to a chair with his wife on one side and Mrs Sterling on the other. Mrs Sterling stares out blankly, seeing nothing. It's as if she's shutting down in response to everything that's happened to them. De Wolff looks at professor Magnussen sitting across from him. He is obviously frightened, and de Wolff can understand why. De Wolff looks round the wide circle of chairs counting the number of people. He counts sixteen; he and his wife, Mrs Sterling, Dr Reynolds, Magnussen, the captain, the mate, the cook, two sailors and six divers. Bob, Jessica and Andy are not there, and neither is Sterling. In the middle of the circle is a chess table. De Wolff realises with a shiver that, in chess, each player has sixteen pieces at his disposal.

Meanwhile, René is trying hard to get untied. The rope is relatively thin, but it's strong, and it cuts deeply into his flesh. The chair he's on seems to be screwed to the floor, and he's unable to move it at all. Mortimer set up this scene quickly after initially locking them up elsewhere.

De Wolff thinks back to what happened to them after they were forced into the helicopter. The helicopter flew over the headland, and the moonlit landscape was made visible through the windows. It would have looked beautiful under other circumstances, but instead, it just looked threatening. No sign of life. No one that could come to their aid. The helicopter landed on a large concrete floodlit platform. It didn't take the professor long to realise that this was the abandoned mine, although clearly, it had been transformed into a well-organised robbers' den. He couldn't tell what Mortimer was using the mine for, and he doubted it would be of much help anyway. He imagined the mine to be the perfect place for the gang — seldom anyone there, but the old roads still passable using heavy trucks. It didn't surprise the professor when he entered the main hall of the large building and saw the trucks — huge beasts with broad tyres that would have little difficulty on the poorly maintained roads.

In the main hall, they were reunited with Sterling and his gang who showed little of their former bravado. They were all taken under heavy guard to a side room which looked like it had once been the miners' changing room. On the ceiling hung cages where the miners could store their clothes while they were underground. Each cage had a steel wire that went to a scaffold in the middle of the hall where the cages could be lowered. Steel benches were installed along the walls, and this was where the expedition members were told to sit down. In low spirits, they all did as they were told except for René who stayed on his feet, and once their captors left, he began to prowl around with the energy of a caged lion.

First, he went round all the doors rattling them to see if he could force his way out, but they were all locked and made of steel, so even René had no hope of getting through them. After that, the French giant moved on to examine the windows, but they were all situated up near the ceiling. That didn't stop René.

"Lift me up in one of the cages," he shouted to the dive team. The men immediately understood what he was planning, and after searching through the steel cables for a while, they found one connected to a cage near a window. They lowered it, and once René was clinging to the outside, they pulled it fifty feet or so up to the high ceiling. If René was afraid of heights, you couldn't tell. The cage came right alongside a fairly large window, and René laughed triumphantly. It would be no problem to knock out the glass.

His first instinct was to smash it with his fist, but just as he was about to do so, he realised the glass might seriously injure him. He ripped a curtain away from its hooks and wrapped it around his hand. Down below, the others watched with their hearts in their mouths as René swung around on the cage holding on with only one hand.

René thumped the glass with his fist, but to his surprise, it didn't crack. He tried again, but his fist simply glanced off the glass without leaving as much as a scratch behind. René threw the curtain down and attacked the window ferociously using his bare fists. He continued until blood dripped from his knuckles, but still, the stubborn window refused to yield. It was made of thick safety glass, and even with a hammer, René wouldn't have been able to put a hole in it. There was nothing for him to do but allow himself to be lowered down again. Back at ground level, he kicked at the doors furiously.

Sterling wasn't looking cheerful either. "I should have listened to you," he said to Mrs de Wolff at one point.

"You're too late with that admission," Mrs de Wolff responded fiercely. "You and your crazy plans to attack an organised gang of criminals with a handful of sailors." Sterling let the criticism roll over him without response.

It wasn't long before some men came to get them — that is, most of them. Bob and Jessica were made to stay behind with Andy in the changing room. Jessica made a desperate attempt to go with her parents, but she was pushed roughly back by one of Mortimer's men. De Wolff almost attacked him, but he made himself focus on the machine guns and remember he didn't stand a chance. They were taken to the large hall where the circle of chairs was, and in no time at all, each person was strapped to one of the seats. Since then they have simply been waiting for whatever is going to happen next.

A door opens. Mortimer enters holding a bundle of papers, and Sterling follows. Earlier, Mortimer took the billionaire to his office to talk. Apparently, the conversation hasn't done the wealthy American much good. His face is ashen, and he looks ill. Mortimer puts his hand on Sterling's shoulder and gently pushes him towards the chessboard that stands in the middle of the circle. He pushes the billionaire into a chair beside it.

"Ladies and gentlemen," he says, looking triumphantly round the circle, "we're going to play a game, the game of death or dollars. I've just explained the rules to Mr Sterling who didn't like the game, but unfortunately, he's not in a position to object. I'll explain the game to you as well because, inadvertently, you're also going to be involved. Here on the table is a chess board. Sterling and I are both keen chess players. Sterling is going to be white, and I'll be black. I thought that was the most appropriate. On the board are sixteen pieces. Together you make sixteen people, and here in my hand, I have sixteen IOUs that all belong to Mr Sterling; his stores; shipyards; railways; shareholdings. Sterling and I will play chess. When he wins a piece, he gets back one of his IOUs. He can choose to keep, for example, his stores. If I win a piece, then I win the life of one of his expedition members" — he pulls a large revolver from his jacket — "whom I will shoot dead," he finishes coolly. He slowly moves round the circle turning his weapon on each of the expedition members, and professor Magnussen finds himself shaking.

"You can't do that," he whispers.

Apparently, this is what Mortimer has been waiting for.

"Maybe I won't do it," he says slowly, "it depends on Mr Sterling. When I win one of your lives, I will give Mr Sterling a choice. If he signs one of the IOUs, then he also saves one of your lives. However, you must remember that Hudson Sterling is a tough businessman, and sometimes to get to the top, you have to step on people on the way up, is that not right, Mr Sterling? "

Sterling doesn't answer. He is sitting behind the chess table with his head bowed.

"I'll take your silence as agreement," laughs Mortimer. "I'll play for Mr Sterling's possessions as detailed in these IOUs, and Mr Sterling can play for the same or your lives. We'll see what is dearest to his heart. Sterling, shall we begin?"

Sterling isn't quite defeated yet. His head snaps up, and his eyes spark. "I will not play," he breathes. "Never!"

"Well, it seems you want to play the hard way," laughs Mortimer.

He snatches up his revolver and walks to the chair where Mrs Sterling is sitting.

"The two children and Andy, the traitor, are not involved in this game, so I have three spare players. We could easily lose a couple here to demonstrate that I'm not bluffing." He points his gun at Mrs Sterling who looks at the barrel in terror.

"No!" she screams.

Mortimer looks at Sterling.

"I'll play, I'll play!" he stammers.

Mortimer smiles. "That's the spirit!" he chuckles. "You're white, so you may start."

Jessica and Bob sit on a bench in the changing room while Andy paces back and forth.

"Where would they have taken mum and dad?" asks Jessica.

Of course Bob doesn't know, and he doesn't bother to answer. He shrugs his shoulders and continues racking his brains for a way for them all to escape. Suddenly, there's a tapping sound from above their heads. Andy is the first to hear it and stops mid-stride. The tapping comes again, more insistently, and Bob and Jessica hear it this time too. Bob looks in the direction the sound's coming from, and high above their heads, he sees a face flattened against the glass.

"What in the world?!" he whispers. "Eric!"

He points up and Jessica sees him too. She jumps to her feet cheering, "Eric! Eric!"

Eric sits above them and peers down through the dirty window. He used a fire ladder to climb to the top and then found that there was a kind of boardwalk with a handrail that ran round the entire roof allowing him to get close to the windows. He saw the helicopters arriving a while ago and wasn't surprised to see the expedition members climbing out. He wanted to run to his parents but controlled himself realising that he was the only one who could do anything for them. He quickly hid himself again, with the intention of finding out where the others would be imprisoned, but accessing the mine wasn't as easy as he expected. All the doors were locked, and the only light came from some faint rays high above his head. He wondered if there might be a window up there he could look through, and after some searching, he found the old rusty fire escape. Now he's on his knees in front of the glass looking down at Bob and Jessica.

Jessica springs to her feet and waves at him. He waves frantically back wondering how he can get them out. The windows are very high, and he doesn't dare call them as on a quiet night like this his voice will easily be heard down below. Bob wasn't born yesterday and understands Eric's dilemma. He walks to the scaffold where the steel cables come out and catches hold of the cable attached to the cage René used. He pulls it a few times, and when Eric sees the cage moving, he catches on to Bob's idea. He gives him a thumbs up. If he smashes the window, they can get out using the cage. He pulls his hand back into the sleeve of his jersey and pounds on the glass. Nothing. The glass is much more stubborn than it looks; he needs a rock or something. He makes a gesture to show that he's going away and then heads back down the fire ladder. He searches around on the ground until he catches sight of an iron bar. Surely that would take out the window. He hurries back up and with a victorious gesture shows the captives the piece of iron. He gestures to them to move aside to avoid being hit by flying glass splinters and then knocks the glass hard. The thump can be heard down below, but nothing happens. Eric hits the window harder, but again nothing happens. Finally, in desperation, Eric uses all of his strength to lash out at the window, but even that is not enough to crack the glass. He leans back angrily against the handrail. Far below him, three pairs of eyes are looking upward in disappointment. They can't unblock their escape route, not even with an iron bar.

"Hey," Jessica suddenly shouts, "I have an idea! Bob, lower the cage."

Bob looks at her with a puzzled expression. "What are you going to do?"

"Wait and see. I'm not sure if it will work or not."

Curious, Bob brings down the cage, and Jessica climbs on to the outside and holds on tightly. Bob and Andy grab the chain and hoist Jessica up. Moments later, she hangs in front of a surprised-looking Eric. Eric shrugs his shoulders and points at the window, but Jessica shakes her head. Being painstakingly careful not to look down, she holds on even more tightly with her left hand as she lets go with her right. On her finger sparkles the diamond ring that, according to her father, can cut glass. She once saw a demonstration in a DIY store about how to cut glass. They showed how to use a glass cutter to mark the glass, then how to tap until a crack appeared, and then finally, how the glass would break where the marks were made. The question was whether her diamond could function as a glass cutter. Carefully Jessica puts her fist on the glass. Now comes the tricky part as she has to use force and that's not easy dangling from the cage. Her ring finger glides over the glass, but the tiny scratch it makes will not be enough. This isn't going to work. She looks at the window frame. Along the lower edge there is a narrow ledge that she could stand on, but she needs a handhold somewhere else. She looks along the top edge and sees a heavy steel curtain rail. She reaches out a hand and grabs on to it, and then she abandons the cage for the ledge. The cage swings away and then continues to swing violently back and forth. It won't be easy to reach it again. With small beads of sweat on her forehead, she looks down. She's so high! If she falls from here, she'll be lucky if all she breaks is a limb. She can't think about it. She sinks down a little so she can reach the lower window frame. That would be the best one to take out as it would be the easiest one to climb through. Eric is watching tensely, still no idea what his sister is up to. He thinks she's intending to try and break the glass, and he's aware that it isn't going to work. Jessica puts her fist against the glass again and slowly pulls the diamond across it. It makes a deep scratch. She beckons Eric closer.

"Tap the glass behind the scratch!" she shouts. Eric shrugs and holds his hands behind his ears, unable to hear anything through the thick glass. Jessica uses gestures to try and make it clear, but Eric still isn't sure what she's getting at. Jessica bites her lip, and then suddenly Eric gets it! With the tip of the iron bar he taps behind the scratch, and Jessica watches tensely. At first, nothing happens. Then suddenly, there's a strange noise, and a large crack appears on the glass.

"Yes!" she cheers. Quickly she puts her fist on the glass again. She makes three more scratches as close to the frame as possible so that the whole window will fall out. Eric hits the stubborn glass again. Andy and Bob watch nervously down below having figured out what Jessica is doing.

Bob bites the nail of his thumb. "Is it working?" he calls up, but Jessica is working too intently to even listen. Eric pounds the glass, and a new crack starts. Another hit and then suddenly, it goes very fast, as if the glass realises that it has lost the battle. The whole section comes loose, but it doesn't fall out of the frame. Eric knows how to deal with it. Gesturing for Jessica to go as far to the side as possible, he turns and holds tightly to the handrail and then kicks with his heel against the glass. Three kicks are enough to knock the glass out, and it falls slowly to the ground before smashing into tiny fragments. What a noise! Bob looks anxiously towards the door, but nobody seems to have heard.

Jessica is now squeezing herself through the gap. The hole is large enough to allow her slender shape through, though there isn't much to hold on to, and it's a long way down. As soon as she's outside, she throws her arms around Eric's neck, and together they do a little dance on the dark roof.

Down below, Bob and Andy have been busy lowering the cage again. With all his strength, Andy starts to pull Bob up feeling that every time he changes his grip, the wire will slip through his fingers. Slowly Bob sees the escape hole in the window getting closer, and when the cage is near enough, Eric leans in through the window to grab Bob and help take some of the weight from Andy. The help is more than welcome to Andy who feels as if his arms are going to be wrenched from their sockets. Bob soon makes it to the window ledge, and he's about to slip out when he remembers Andy down below.

"Lower the cage again!" he calls down.

"You'll never get me up." says Andy. "You three go!"

"No way!" says Bob. "The three of us will get you up together."

Still a little hesitant, Andy lowers the cage back down.

"I'm not sure this is going to work," Bob says as he stands on the ledge and pulls the cable in towards them. Eric and Jessica each put out an arm and grab the cable too. The three of them pull, but it's not easy because they need to hold on to stop themselves from falling, so they can each only use one hand. Their first attempts fail, as whenever Andy is three feet or so up, one of them lets go of the rope at the wrong time, and the American falls back down. Then Bob takes the lead calling out the name of the person whose turn it is to release their grip and grab the rope further down. This system works, and Andy starts rising slowly. He holds on anxiously to the side of the cage; if something goes wrong at this height, it's a long way to fall. However, nothing goes wrong, and a few minutes later, Andy is reaching up to grab the bottom edge of the window. Then gripping the top, he finally pulls himself through. He breathes a huge sigh of relief.

The four of them stand together on the roof. Okay, so they're free. But what should they do now?

Far below them, the game of death or dollars is still being played. It's Sterling's move, and the game isn't shaping up well for him. No matter what he does next, he is going to lose a piece. After a long hesitation, he decides to give up a castle. Mortimer responds quickly and takes the castle with his bishop.

"Well, well," he says with satisfaction, "a castle! A solid figure. I think the closest match we have here is the leader of your diving team, René du Nord."

He grabs his gun, and Sterling sees that it is a Smith and Wesson 5946; a nine mm Parabellum with fifteen rounds in the magazine; a deadly weapon.

"A solid guy is worth a solid IOU," Mortimer continues. He grabs one of the papers. "Yes, this is a fun one: your oil tanker fleet." He pushes the paper under the nose of the billionaire and points with the barrel of his gun to the bottom of the page. "You sign here, unless you feel your tanker fleet is worth more than the life of our tough, frog eating friend?"

"I will not sign," Sterling says.

"All right," says Mortimer, shrugging his shoulders. He walks over to René who is glaring back, but René's tough guy attitude doesn't last long as he feels the cold steel against his ear. Sweat breaks out and flows over his forehead in thin rivulets, and he looks at the billionaire with big eyes.

"Mr Sterling, please!" he whispers. Sterling's hands have clenched into fists.

Mortimer puts his finger on the trigger. "Life is so fragile," he says philosophically, "a couple of seconds, and it might all be over. There will come a day when you'll die and have to leave all your belongings behind. I'd rather have your tankers now and let this poor Frenchman live, but it's your decision! His fate is in your hands. Tell me now! "

Sterling pulls the paper towards him fiercely and grabs the pen. With powerful strokes, he signs it.

"It still has no legal validity," he can't resist saying.

"Oh, no?" Mortimer laughs. "We'll see about that. I will not let you go before I'm sure I have the lot, you can count on that. On with the game! It's your move!"

René is doubled over, and for a moment, de Wolff thinks he has lost consciousness, but then he realises this isn't the case. The large shoulders are shaking, and tears are dripping down his nose to the ground. The Frenchman has just had his Waterloo, and de Wolff feels only pity for him. De Wolff looks angrily at Mortimer, who grins slyly back.

Chapter 18: The counterattack

"LOOK AT THAT," says Eric. He points in the direction of the harbour, and the others turn to see what he's looking at. The four of them are still standing on the roof and have a good view of the abandoned village and the harbour beyond. Eric spots the Aquatic Dream which has been moored just behind the Rubicon.

"Couldn't we get back on board?" Eric suggests. "Then we could radio for help."

Andy shakes his head. "Sterling threw the emergency radio overboard and shot the main radio. Mortimer's men finished the job, and it's beyond repair now."

Now Eric understands why he couldn't contact them towards the end of his time on the Rubicon.

Bob is thinking through how they could call for help and comes up with the only other possible solution. "Mortimer's boat also has a radio on board," he says.

Andy's not sure it'll do much good. "You were there when your father had a policeman in Hebron on the radio," he says, "and the guy didn't believe a word we said."

"He's not the only policeman in the world." Jessica doesn't want to give up. "Anyone got a better idea?" There is silence from the other three. "Well, come on then," she says, "let's go get that radio!"

They make their way down the ladder and through the deserted village in single file. When they reach the port, they can see Mortimer's men aboard the Aquatic Dream. Using the cover of the shadows, they manage to draw close to see what the men are up to. A couple of them are trying to force the door to the armoury, but the steel door is well built and does not yield. After fifteen minutes, they give up and abandon the boat. To the surprise of the hidden party, no guard is left behind, which is a stroke of luck. They wait until they're sure the men have all gone, and then they creep toward the gangway of the Rubicon. Andy is leading the way when he suddenly stops dead in his tracks, and Jessica walks straight into him.

"What?" she whispers.

"There's someone on the deck," Andy replies softly. "I saw the tip of his cigarette glowing."

The four of them peer at the boat, and then the others see it too. Just the tiniest of lights. The man walks across the deck, and he is suddenly visible, framed against the night sky. He puts a foot on the railing and stares across the water. Mortimer has apparently left him on guard.

"How are we going to get on board?" Eric asks quietly.

"Leave that to me," says Bob confidently. "If you hide under the gangway, I'll lure him off the boat."

"How are you going to do that?" Andy wants to know.

"You'll see," is the only answer he gets.

Bob has already disappeared into the darkness. The other three do what he says; they creep over to the gangway and crawl underneath it. Bob feels around with his feet in the darkness until he uncovers a loose stone. Picking it up, he runs to a storage hut nearby and hurls it through the window. The glass smashes and scatters across the concrete floor, and Bob looks over to see if the guard has heard. It seems he has, as he turns in the direction the sound has come from and stares out into the darkness, but he makes no move to leave the ship. Bob smashes a second window, and the man descends a little way down the gangway. Finally, Bob knocks out a third pane and runs back towards the village, and the man gives chase.

Andy, Jessica and Eric hear the guard pass above their heads as he runs down the gangway, and they wait until he's disappeared between the houses. Then they move quickly.

"Let's take the emergency radio," Andy suggests, "then we can go to the Aquatic Dream where there's no guard."

They rush to the bridge where, even in the dark, Eric can find the cupboard easily. Luckily, the radio has been put back where it belongs, and moments later, Andy has it under his arm, and they abandon ship. As they walk along the quay, Andy freezes again, and this time it's Eric who bumps into him, almost knocking the radio into the water. A shadowy figure is coming towards them. Jessica inhales sharply.

"Hey, folks," says a voice, "don't panic, it's only me!"

"Bob," sighs Eric in relief, "where did the guard go?"

"I don't know, I lost him somewhere between the houses."

"Let's go to the radio room of the Aquatic Dream!" Andy suggests. "We can use the radio there without being disturbed."

They quickly make their way aboard and once in the radio room, Andy puts the device on the table. Everything would be so much easier if they could put on a light, but fortunately, Andy can work the radio in the dark.

"Who are you going to call?" Eric wants to know.

"I'll try the police in Hebron again first," Andy says. "I can remember the frequency off the top of my head." He turns on the device and puts on the headphones.

"Hebron Police Department," comes a voice from the unit.

"Yes!" Jessica cheers and then quietens to listen. Will they be believed this time? Andy asks for Norris, and to his amazement, the policeman is there within seconds. Andy updates him on what has happened — without much hope that the agent will listen — but Norris reacts very differently this time.

"I believe you," he says. "I'm sorry for doubting you before, but you must admit that your story didn't sound very credible. However, after I heard you being captured over the radio, I contacted the Sterling Company and after some hesitation on their part, they confirmed the details of the expedition."

Andy is deeply relieved. "What should we do?" he asks.

"We've been busy here," Norris says. "Not so far away from you, north east of Fort Chimo, is a secret commando training centre. I raised the alarm there, and there are now four helicopters full of highly trained commandos on their way to you."

"How long will it be before they get here?" Andy wants to know.

"Less than an hour," comes the response.

"Yes!" Jessica calls for the umpteenth time, slapping Bob enthusiastically on the back.

"What shall we do now?" asks Andy.

"See if you can create a bit of panic," says Norris, "the more confusion on the ground the easier it will be for the commandos to move in when they arrive."

"Okay," Andy promises, "we'll do our best."

Bob, Eric and Jessica have been able to hear the policeman as Andy has only used one side of the headphones and left the other clear for them to listen. Bob is already working on a plan.

"We could start by setting the village on fire," he suggests.

"That sounds like a good idea," says Andy, "but I have an even better one."

"What's your idea?" the others want to know.

"Just come with me," grins the American. He leaves the radio room, and they walk out on deck. They're unlikely to be discovered here, but they keep their eyes open nonetheless. Andy goes directly to the armoury door.

"If we could get that open, we could create some major panic," says Bob.

"My thoughts exactly," says Andy.

"But you'll never get into it!" says Eric. "You can't get past the lock."

Andy waves his fingers in the air. "You might be surprised, my boy!" he says. He leans in slightly, and his fingers dance over the keys; then he turns the wheel, and the door swings open. Eric's mouth drops open.

"How's that possible?" he asks aloud.

"I spent whole nights sitting by the radio; the door was a pleasant distraction; actually, it was easier than I thought; even the first time, I had it open within an hour."

"Fantastic!" says Bob. "We can each grab a gun and start shooting. That will definitely cause panic. The village is deserted, so it doesn't matter what we hit."

Andy shakes his head. "We can't just start shooting at random, Mortimer's men will be after us in minutes, and those guys are really dangerous. If they see us, we're in serious trouble. We have to cause havoc without being seen."

"How do we do that then?" asks Jessica.

"I don't know exactly," Andy admits. "Let's start by seeing what we've got in here."

They all walk into Sterling's armoury and have a look round. The main attraction seems to be the Sniper Rifle.

"I know how to shoot it," says Bob, "and it has a long range. We could drag it right out of the village and up the mountainside. That way they wouldn't be able to tell where the shots were coming from. By the time they figured it out, the helicopters would be here."

Andy nods. "That's not such a bad idea," he says, "but you watch where you're shooting! Never near people. Shoot glass and other stuff that will make a lot of noise."

Bob nods and lifts the heavy piece of equipment to the ground.

"I'll go with you!" Jessica decides.

"Fine!" Bob agrees.

"Then Eric and I will team up," says Andy.

Bob shows Jessica where the rounds are, and Jessica fills her pockets with them. There are also dark sweaters on the shelves, and they each pull one on before disappearing into the night. Apparently, the guard is still searching because there's no sign of him on the other boat. They need to be careful not to bump into him.

"Shall we go to that tower?" Jessica asks softly.

"I already thought of that," says Bob, "but it seems a bit risky. If they figure out we're up there, then there's nowhere for us to escape to. We'd be better going out of the village and getting a safe distance away. This gun will easily shoot over a kilometre."

They leave the port and dodge their way through the village. Before long, they reach a beach and can move at speed because the tide is out and the sand hard. They jog along the water's edge, although Bob finds it hard going with the heavy weapon.

"Can you manage?" asks Jessica, seeing that her brother is struggling.

Bob grimaces. "We don't have to go much further," he pants. "We can climb up that hill over there."

He indicates a hill a hundred yards or so away, and they head over to it. The slope is very steep, and Bob is relieved when they reach the top.

"I feel like my arms have stretched a good few inches," he groans as he puts down the gun. From the top, they have a good view of the abandoned village. Bob unfolds the tripod and sets up the rifle.

"Aren't you afraid to shoot that thing?" Jessica asks, viewing it with dislike.

"A little bit," Bob admits, "it's a dangerous weapon, I'd never forgive myself if I accidentally hit someone with it."

"What are you going to aim for?" Jessica wants to know.

"I'm not sure yet," replies Bob. "I'll have a look through the sights and wait and see what Eric and Andy are going to do."

He gets behind the weapon and lies down on his belly while Jessica sits on a stone and watches. He adjusts the sights but can't see anything. He moves the barrel around, and he is just beginning to wonder if it's broken, when he sees the moon shining on a rooftop. It seems so close it's as if he were on the roof itself! Now that he's got something in his sights to orientate himself, he locates the port and aims the gun at the front boat. Suddenly, he sees the guard again. The man has returned to his post on the boat. Bob brings him into focus until he can see him clearly in the cross hairs of the sights. If the weapon was loaded, Bob could shoot now, and the man would be taken out like a skittle hit with a bowling ball. Bob moves the sights until he is looking at the bridge; a few rounds through the windows ought to cause a bit of confusion.

"Do you have the rounds?" he asks Jessica. His sister digs a box from her pocket and shoves it into his hands, and Bob loads the rifle. He aims for the windows again.

"Well, come on Andy," he says, "start something!"

At that very moment Andy is walking with Eric through the deserted streets of the village. Eric knows exactly where the helicopters are and leads Andy to the concrete landing platform. They crouch down behind a crumbling wall and look over the top. There's no-one there. Andy puts down the backpack he's been carrying.

"Stay here," he says as he takes two mines from the bag.

"Do you know how those things work?" Eric wonders, a little worried.

"I spent a lot of time in the military," says Andy. "This is nothing."

"Are you really going to blow up those helicopters?" says Eric. "Won't you get into trouble?"

"If someone has a problem with it, I'll send them to Mr Sterling," Andy replies. "I'm sure he'll gladly cover the cost of the helicopters if we get him out of here unscathed."

Keeping low, he runs across the landing platform and hoists himself up into one of the cockpits. He puts the mine convex side up on one of the chairs, and checking his watch, sets it to go off in seven minutes. He waits until the red digital numbers start to count down and then quickly runs to the other chopper and sets up the second mine to go off in five minutes. Then he runs back to Eric.

"Come on," he says, "we'll put some more of these in the village!" Eric grabs the backpack and follows Andy to one of the houses.

"Give me a mine!" says the young American to his Dutch comrade, and in no time, they lay mines in four of the cottages and run out of the town towards the hills. Andy checks his watch, and once they are clear of the village, he puts out a hand and stops Eric. From where they stand, they're high enough to see the helicopters in the distance. As they watch, the silence of the night is ripped apart by an explosion. The cockpit doors are blown off the helicopter as the clouds of fire spill out. The blades fly up in the air, and the rotor turns strangely on its axis before crashing to the ground. Pieces of camouflage net fly in all directions, and there is the sound of debris raining down. High flames come out from the wreck. The whole thing is so dramatic that Eric is still staring at the devastation with his mouth open when the second helicopter blows up with equal force. The yellow-red flames left after the explosions light up the scene as the main doors of the base fly open and men rush out.

"Let's get out of here," says Andy, pulling Eric by the shoulder. Together they run up the hillside and away from the chaos they've created.

"I wonder what Bob's doing," Eric says.

"He might have been waiting for us to make the first move," supposes Andy.

"I don't think he'll have missed it!" chuckles Eric.

"Good grief!" says Bob as the sound of the explosion rolls up the slope. They watch as below them, the first helicopter dies a fiery death, followed shortly by the second.

Jessica jumps to her feet, startled. "That must have been Andy and Eric," she says.

"Must have been," says Bob. He peers through the sights where he can see the guard standing at the railing, weapon in hand, watching the red glow that hangs over the village. Bob aims the gun and fires at the large panoramic windows, and the glass shatters. The startled guard dives behind a box on the deck and looks with bewilderment at the bridge just as a second glass panel shatters, and the glass rains down on him. Bob watches with satisfaction, and then his attention is diverted by a third explosion. When he looks through the sights, he sees that one of the houses in the village is ablaze. There are already men alongside the helicopters.

"It looks like someone's thrown a stone into an anthill," says Jessica.

Another explosion shakes the village as house number two goes up.

"It's like a warzone down there," says Bob. "I hope Andy knows what he's doing, because if those guys get hold of him, he's a dead man."

Chapter 19. Mortimer

"WHAT WAS THAT?!" Mortimer jumps up from his chair. The others — still tied to their chairs — look surprised. A moment later, one of Mortimer's men bursts into the room.

"Mr Mortimer!" he yells. "The helicopters!"

Furious, the gang leader jumps up and runs to the door. He arrives just in time to see one of the buildings in the village going up. To his right, he sees the burning wrecks of the helicopters.

"How can this be?" he roars. He turns around and looks at the circle of people. "We'll continue our game later", he hisses, "but with stricter rules!"

He gives orders to some of his men to lock up the prisoners again and then dashes out to find out exactly what is going on. The men hastily force the prisoners back to the changing rooms, only to find, to their amazement, that the room is empty.

Mortimer is quickly informed, and in no time at all, the gang leader is back inside.

"That wretched radio freak!" Mortimer mutters through clenched teeth. Then he turns to professor de Wolff. "I think I know what's happened," he says, his eyes flashing. "That youngest son of yours has got them out somehow. We're now fighting a treacherous radio technician and three children. Well, that shouldn't be too hard. I'll get them, and then I'll make you all pay for this. You can count on that, professor!"

De Wolff says nothing back; he suspects that Mortimer is right. Deep down he's proud; proud of his sons and his daughter who have proven in the past that they can stand strong under pressure. However, his pride is overshadowed by fear. Mortimer knows who his opponents are; how long will they be able to hold out against him?

Bob is still lying behind the sniper rifle and wonders what his next move should be. He's shot out nearly all of the Rubicon's windows and isn't sure where to shoot next; he doesn't want to hit anybody accidentally. His gaze wanders over the main building, and he thinks of his parents trapped somewhere inside.

What will be happening to them now? Mortimer will probably have locked them back up in the changing room. Will they notice the broken pane and realise there's a way out? He aims the sights at the main building. He can see the walkway round the roof, but it's too dark to make out the broken window. A plan suddenly flashes into his head. Wouldn't the sniper rifle be able to take out the strengthened windows in the changing room? He decides to test out the theory straight away. He knows roughly where the broken window is; he mustn't shoot anywhere near there just in case anyone is trying to scramble out. He selects a window further along, and then biting his lip, he pulls the trigger. The round goes straight through the window, and he can see the glass smashing to pieces. It works! He quickly shoots again until he empties the magazine. Pane after pane, the glass shatters. It won't be hard for them to see the way out now!

De Wolff draws his wife to him as suddenly there is a deafening bang overhead, and glass fragments rain down on them. Wham! Another window shatters into pieces, and a bullet flies between the cages over their heads. They all look up, their hands raised protectively over their heads. Six windows are taken out, and then it goes quiet.

"Why did they do that?" asks one of the divers.

Sterling picks up a piece of glass. "That's not ordinary glass," he says. "You couldn't shoot through that with regular bullets, but it was definitely a bullet that took out the windows — a grenade would have torn the whole frame out."

"The sniper rifle?" René suggests.

Sterling shrugs. "Who could have got it out of the vault?" he asks.

"Could Andy have managed that?" says de Wolff.

"Andy?" Sterling says with obvious disdain. Clearly, his opinion of the traitor is still very low. "He wouldn't know how to shoot the rifle," he replies.

"My son would," says de Wolff. Sterling remembers the shooting session on the ocean and looks questioningly at the professor.

"I think Andy and Bob have just shown us the way out," says the Dutch scholar.

René is already looking appraisingly upwards. "We can get up there," he says.

Mortimer is looking with fury at the burned helicopters.

"Comb the village!" he shouts to his men. "They've hidden themselves here somewhere."

He is mistaken. Eric and Andy have followed the light trail from the rounds Bob has fired and have joined Bob and Jessica on the hill.

"You can stop shooting," says Andy. "If we stay here, they'll never find us.

At the same time, a dull hum can be heard from the horizon.

Startled, Mortimer looks up at the sky. Four heavy helicopters are flying over the ridge. With a thunderous roar, they fly right over the stunned men while the pilots assess the situation on the ground. They weren't sure how much to believe of the report they received over the radio, but even a child could see something's going on down there. A few of Mortimer's men have the presence of mind to fire at the aircraft. The bullets don't cause any damage, but the commandos immediately realise how serious the situation is. They grab their weapons and prepare to move out as soon as the aircrafts are on the ground. The pilots land in the darkness, well beyond the range of Mortimer's guns. The tailgates are lowered, and dozens of commandos stream out. Mortimer sees that, between the four helicopters, more than a hundred men come out. He knows he doesn't stand a chance, and grinding his teeth with rage, he makes his decision.

"Evacuate!" he growls to the men who are running around near him. "You know the escape routes."

He's the first back into the main building, and he runs to the back of the hall where there is a huge steel door. Behind it lie the passages from the former mine, leading into the mountain. Along the side are a dozen or so large motorbikes. Mortimer jumps into the saddle of one and kicks the engine into life. The noise reverberates round the rough walls of the passages as he takes off. A second motor, and then a third, ride off into the darkness of the abandoned mine. All the bikes soon leave, and the remaining men run on foot into the mine using torches to light the way.

Mortimer knows his way through the underground labyrinth. A long way ahead, one of these tunnels will exit into the middle of the wilderness, and there he will escape. Furious, he rides at a death-defying speed through the tunnels. They haven't seen the last of him. He'll have his revenge on Sterling. Better still, he'll have his revenge on the Dutch professor and his wretched children. When he gets out of this mess and back on his feet, they'll be the first people he comes for.

"I'll get you, de Wolff!" he shouts angrily. His voice can be heard above the noise of the engine and echoes back into the hall. "I'll get you!"

The battle outside the mine is short. Once Mortimer's men see they are heavily outnumbered, the word spreads quickly. "Get out! Into the mine!" In no time at all, the commandos have the situation under control. Up on the roof, a few men do a victory dance; it's René and the divers. They managed to get out the windows, but it was difficult, and by the time they were out, the battle was over. The others have an easier route out after the commandos free them from their prison. De Wolff introduces himself to the leader who is built like a tank. A nice guy, as long as you're on his side, which fortunately de Wolff is. He gives the Canadian a summary of what's happened over the last few hours.

Andy and the children watch from the hill, and as soon as they see it's safe, they come down. The de Wolff family are overjoyed to be reunited again. Eric flies to his mother and throws his arms around her neck. He can feel tears pouring down his face as all the pent up emotion of the last few days is finally released. Mr de Wolff puts his arms around Bob and Jessica.

"Good thing I knew how to shoot that gun," Bob can't help saying. Mr de Wolff doesn't agree, but he's not going to talk about it now. There will be plenty of time to talk later. De Wolff suddenly longs for home and their cozy living room in the Groningen Singels. While they're still standing around, one of the helicopters prepares for take-off, and the commander walks over in their direction.

"A lot of the gang members escaped through the mine," he explains, "we're going to take the helicopter and see if we can catch them on the other side of the hill where the passages are likely to lead out. Meanwhile, I'd like you to come with me so you can give me more information about everything that has happened."

The whole group goes inside the main hall again, and they listen to one another's stories. The de Wolff family and Andy do most of the talking. René, the divers, and the crew don't say much; they realise that they were mistaken and that those who they thought were cowards have turned out to be the heroes. Sterling says nothing and seems to hear little of what is being said. He sits on a chair with his wife pressed against him and stares continuously at the chessboard lying on the ground. His mind is in tumult.

"Are you planning to leave with the expedition ship?" asks the commander. "You're welcome to fly out with us."

The professor wants to get away as soon as possible and chooses to fly with the Canadians. He's happy to wash his hands of the entire Titanic Expedition. In retrospect, he wishes he never got involved in the first place. He says as much to Sterling, and the billionaire just nods, hardly hearing what is being said. De Wolff sees that he is still staring with glassy eyes at the chessboard. De Wolff puts his hand on the American's shoulder, then he bends down, picks up the black king, and presses it into the billionaire's hands.

"Today you have beaten the black king," he says, "but there is another black king who you can't beat on your own. Not with all your weapons. There will come a day when you really have to leave all your earthly possessions behind, and you will not have anything with which to pay your debts to the black king. The only one who can help you then is The King, with a capital letter. The King who has conquered the world without violence! You will understand this if you really are a Christian. Keep this black king as a reminder of what I've just said to you." Then he turns around and leaves the room with his wife and children.

The de Wolffs are taken by the Canadians to Fort Chimo, and from there they take the first plane home. Their belongings will be sent on.

De Wolff stares out of the window of the plane. It's a clear day, and underneath them, the sunlight shines across the Atlantic. The same ocean where the Titanic disappeared. Mrs de Wolff guesses what he's thinking about and sits close to him with a hand on his knee. De Wolff feels her shoulder against his.

In front of him he can see a strand of Jessica's hair spilling over the airplane seat, and behind him he hears his two boys laugh as Bob says something funny.

It's at this moment that he realises the adventure is over, and the five of them are still safely together. A warm feeling spreads over him, and he visibly relaxes.

"When we get home, the five of us will do something fun," he smiles. "A short break or something."

"Fine," laughs Mrs de Wolff looking a bit naughty, "as long as it's not anywhere by the sea!"

The police tell them later that Mortimer has escaped. Professor de Wolff doesn't care much — he's happy to forget his Titanic adventure as quickly as possible.

He may wish to forget, but Mortimer does not.

But that is another story . . .

THE END

Preview - Chapter 1 of 'Chess in the Wilderness'

Read on for the first chapter of

CHESS IN THE WILDERNESS
de Wolff Adventure Series volume 2

Chapter 1. Mortimer runs off

Labrador, Canada

An abandoned mine shaft

DARKNESS. INK BLACK darkness and utter silence.

Then a soft hum, like an angry hornet. A faint patch of light in the distance turns the walls of the mine shaft a ghostly white. The humming becomes stronger, the light brighter, then a motorbike comes flying round the corner, its headlight round and bright. The sound of the heavy terrain engine rumbles through the dark passages, literally deafening. You can just see a black shadow in the saddle bent low over the handlebars.

Mortimer — the rider of the bike — curses aloud, but he can't even hear his own voice. Furious, he grips his hands tighter round the steering wheel, and his eyes blaze darkly. This is a setback. A huge disappointment. This abandoned mine with its labyrinth of passages running deep into the mountains was the perfect cover for his illegal activities in Canada, especially since it was situated next to a small port. How many drugs has he smuggled here over the last few years?! He organised to have motorbikes ready so they could make a quick escape if anything went wrong, but he never thought things might actually go wrong. Well, now they have. He's not sure exactly how they did it, but he is certain that the children of that miserable Dutch professor are to blame. Bitterly certain. How did they manage to get helicopters full of commandos to his mine? His gang were outnumbered, and he had no choice but to tell them to run. He, Mortimer, perhaps the most wanted criminal in the United States, was having to flee and leave everything behind, running like a coward into the mine and then escaping on the bike!

If only he handled it differently! If he just caught the kid who stowed away on board and thrown him into the sea! He had already stolen the vaults of the Titanic from the expedition ship, yet he decided to lure the whole expedition party into the port just so he could get his hands on the billionaire Sterling. He almost did it though. He forced the wealthy businessman to his knees; he had papers giving him control of Sterling's assets; all the power was his! Then suddenly, circling like hawks, those Air Force helicopters appeared in the sky, full of armed soldiers. How did they know about the old mine? Someone ought to have betrayed him, and the only one who could have done it was that son of the Dutch professor. He must have managed to help his brother, sister and that treacherous radioman to escape, and together they succeeded in making contact with the military base.

Again, he gives a roar of rage. His whole organisation in northern Canada has been dismantled. He is not finished yet though, his crime empire has more arms. At the moment, his primary concern is to escape, and that won't be easy now that there are helicopters involved. They will be watching the entire area from the skies, and if they catch sight of him, the game will be over. He can't think like that! His escape plan is good; the route through the passages isn't hard to follow as long ago he had reflective paint put on the walls; he's travelling as fast as he dares, and it is fast. There were more escape bikes ready in the mine, and some of the gang will try to flee using the same route. He wants to stay ahead of them as his chances of remaining undetected are better if he's alone.

Suddenly, he sees the distant twinkling light of a low star. He has reached the exit already, and the tunnel is rapidly widening out. A small and inconspicuous truck is parked at the end of the mine corridor, its tailgate down. In one fluid movement, Mortimer drives up and into the back of the truck and then quickly secures the bike. He jumps down and lifts up the tailgate fastening the locking pins in place.

Running round to the front, he climbs up and slides in behind the wheel. He can hear in the distance the sound of another bike coming. He needs to move fast! If there are others fleeing across the ground, he has a greater chance of escape. He turns the ignition key, and the heavy engine springs to life. On the outside, the van appears to be a rusty vehicle of some hillbilly who lives here in the wilderness, but it hides a modern, powerful engine. There is enough food in the back to last for several days. It shouldn't be difficult to reach civilisation with this vehicle. He quickly takes a look at the compass mounted on the dashboard, and then he drives the truck out. He looks anxiously at the sky, but under the cover of the night, there is nothing to see. Initially, he doesn't dare to put on the headlights, but he soon realises this was a bad decision. In no time at all, he is ploughing through thickets and bumping into rocks. If he continues like this, he's going to get stuck.

Cursing, he turns on the headlights. He realises he's now an easy target to anyone watching from the air, but perhaps they are too busy on the other side of the mountain at the mine. Who knows, maybe they haven't even given chase.

But he is wrong.

By order of the commander, one of the major transport helicopters is already taking off with the pilot, co-pilot, and ten heavily armed soldiers on board. The huge Chinook swings round in the air, and through the open side door, two soldiers with night-vision goggles peer out across the landscape. A few gang members fled on motorbikes into the mine and it's likely there is an escape route through the mountain. If so, they will come out somewhere on the other side unless the tunnel changes direction and re-routes elsewhere. The pilot decides to linger just above the highest point of the ridge. He and the co-pilot look out over the mountain landscape, and the two soldiers with night-vision goggles do the same from the side door. The co-pilot is the first to spot Mortimer's headlights and points down excitedly. He calls over his shoulder to the soldiers in the belly of the aircraft, and the men at the side door spot the truck as well.

"They fled on motorbikes, didn't they?" asks one of the men.

"Who else would be driving out there?" another answers.

"We can't just shoot at innocent people!" says the first.

"We'll move in closer," says the pilot through his headphones.

Suddenly, they see another headlight.

"There is the exit of the mine!" shouts one of the men. The pilot is already making contact with the base, and a moment later, he is talking with the commander himself. There follows a brief conversation.

"We need to chase the truck," he shouts over his shoulder, "the commander suspects that it's the gang leader himself trying to escape. Another helicopter is already in the air and coming to seal off the entrance to the mine."

With a thunderous roar, the heavy helicopter flies over the mountain range and into the valley following right behind Mortimer's small truck.

Mortimer has not yet noticed anything. His full attention is taken up managing driving on the rugged terrain. The truck dances across the bumpy surface, and Mortimer curses softly. Wasn't there once a path here somewhere? An old route to the mine? The small truck crawls up an earthy ridge, and then suddenly, there is the road he was searching for. A wide, bumpy, unpaved path through the wilderness formerly used by heavy transport trucks from the mine. Those vehicles had no trouble with this track, and neither does his truck with its heavy treaded tyres.

The gang leader is pleased to see that he can immediately increase his speed. At this rate, he'll be out of the area before the hunt even starts. He's even confident enough now to turn off the headlights. His eyes take some time to adjust to the darkness, but the moon is high in the sky, and her silver light is enough for him to be able to make out the road. Mortimer is about to give a victory cry when his truck is suddenly caught in a bright circle of light. He hears a heavy pounding above the noise of his engine. He puts down the side window, and sand swirls inside. The heavy pounding becomes stronger, pushing against his chest. With narrowed eyes, he looks upward and sees a helicopter flying right above him, and he pounds his fist on the steering wheel furiously.

Under the helicopter hangs a loudspeaker. "Stop the truck!" orders the voice of the pilot. Mortimer has no intention of doing so. He puts the headlights back on and floors the accelerator.

The pilot sees that the fugitive has no interest in surrendering. He lets the helicopter sweep over the truck, spraying up clouds of dust against the windscreen so that Mortimer is forced to slow down. Then the helicopter flies further in front and remains there, hovering just above the road. Mortimer can see the helicopter in front of him now as it hangs like a giant insect, its bright lights dazzling him.

"Stop the truck!" thunders the voice from the speaker again. "Stop the truck or we will open fire!"

Mortimer is conflicted. He knows their threats are real, but if he stops, they'll catch him. He is high on the list of "most wanted" criminals, he would go to jail for years. Never! He'd rather risk his life than spend the rest of it behind bars. He narrows his eyes, clenches his teeth, and pushes the accelerator down again. The truck heads straight for the helicopter.

"Stop the truck!"

Mortimer doesn't think so. Driving at high speed, he races underneath the helicopter. Dust and grit hit the windscreen like a hailstorm, and the heavy turbulence caused by the two rotors of the helicopter causes the truck to dance across the road. For a moment, Mortimer thinks his vehicle will be blown over, but the high spec engine and heavy treaded tyres prove their worth, and suddenly, he is past the helicopter, and the road is clear again. Mortimer knows they will be back on his tail in a few minutes. If only there was a forest where he could get under cover, but this landscape is harsh and exposed. It's going to be a game of cat and mouse. A game in which Mortimer is the mouse, but he is a determined mouse, and he will not be easily caught.

A discussion is underway in the helicopter about what action to take next. The fugitive in the truck has shown he's not easily intimidated. The soldiers don't take long to reach a decision, and the best marksmen are put at the side door, machine guns ready, while the pilot manoeuvres alongside the fleeing truck.

Mortimer sees the helicopter and instinctively cowers which turns out to be a life saver as a split second later, bullets rain down on the truck. The windscreen shatters, and as bullets pierce through the bonnet, the engine starts to make a strange whining sound. Mortimer shouts out in anger. One of the headlights is hit, and then the helicopter overtakes the truck and flies right in front of it again. Without the protection of the windscreen, the sand and gravel swirl inside like a mini tornado. Mortimer holds up a hand to his face as the gravel hits him and tries not to breathe as he feels the dust entering his lungs. With his other hand he pulls the steering wheel hard round so the truck speeds off the road. The road is slightly higher than the surrounding terrain, and for a moment, the truck is airborne, and then the wheels hit the ground, and the tyres grip the rough road again. The truck ploughs over the uneven terrain, and the engine stutters. Has it been damaged by a bullet? Suddenly there's a bang, and the engine cuts out completely. Mortimer floors the accelerator, but the truck is slowing. He turns the key in the ignition, but the engine won't respond, and within a matter of seconds, the vehicle comes to a full stop.

Mortimer throws the door of the truck open intending to make a run for it, but realises that on foot he'll have no chance against the men in the helicopter. The motorbike! He might have a chance on that! His brain works overtime as he tries to think of something that would slow his pursuers down for a few minutes and give him time to escape. He rushes to the back of the truck and lowers the tailgate. The motorbike has fallen on its side, and it takes all his strength to lift it back up. However, the engine is still warm, and he's relieved to find he has no problem kick-starting it. Just as he's about to drive away, he glances at the helicopter heading in his direction. In a few seconds they'll have him in their spotlight, and he has no protection against their bullets now. Suddenly, a risky plan flashes into his head. He gets off the motorbike. When the circle of light nears the truck, there is no sign of a fugitive fleeing, and the commandos decide to land. As soon as the helicopter is on the ground, the ten heavily armed men jump out of the side door and surround the truck. The leader communicates with the pilot through his flight helmet.

"It looks empty," he says, "we're going in for a closer look."

He gives a signal to two of his men, and they sneak alongside the truck. One hides right next to the door, while the other directs his machine gun inside. "Don't move!"

"Empty!" calls the closest man. He shakes his head as his voice is lost in the roar of the helicopter engine. Would the guy have tried to run off on foot? He doesn't stand a chance. The sun's coming up, and there's nowhere to hide out here.

The leader points to the back of the truck. Could he be hiding in there? It doesn't seem likely, what would be the point? Two other soldiers are already on their way to the tailgate with their guns hanging casually from their shoulders. It strikes them as strange that the locking pins are not in place, but they're still not expecting to find anyone. They lower the tailgate but before they have time to look inside, a motorbike comes flying out knocking them backwards. For a moment, the soldiers are so surprised that they fail to respond, and that gives Mortimer the time he needs to speed out of the lit circle and away.

As soon as he is out of the light, he changes direction swinging deftly to the right, but the leader of the group has rapidly recovered and is already firing into the dark night. Most of the rounds are lost in the wilderness, but one finds its mark and hits Mortimer in the calf. The gang leader shouts out in pain. It feels like his leg is on fire. With great difficulty he manages to keep his cool; he needs to get away from here as quickly as possible; it doesn't matter where. He struggles to stay in the saddle as his wounded leg slips from the pedal. As he rides grimly on, the sky turns from black to dark blue. The sun rises early here; he has to get away from the helicopter. Red spots dance in front of his eyes, and he shakes his head fiercely. Angrily, he realises he can't hold out much longer. Suddenly the wheels of his bike are no longer on the ground, and with a flash of fear, Mortimer recalls that the land out here is scarred with chasms. His stomach seems to rise, and he has the bitter taste of bile in his mouth, as with a terrified cry, he disappears into the depths.

The soldiers have run back to the helicopter, and the pilot swiftly takes the machine straight up. They fly in the direction Mortimer seemed to be heading in without realising he shifted course as soon as he was out of the helicopter's circle of light.

"We lost him!" the pilot calls after a while. The leader stands at the side door and peers through his binoculars desperately trying to pick up the bike's tracks but he knows that at this altitude, and with the poor light, he doesn't have much of a chance.

"Don't go too far!" he shouts through his earpiece to the pilot. "Fly in circles! It's getting lighter, and we might get lucky."

"I think all the luck in the world's with the other guy," grumbles the pilot.

But he is wrong. Mortimer screams as he flies through the air, every moment expecting to hit the rocks and be killed, but the collision never comes. Instead, he suddenly plunges into water. He touches the bottom, but the water is deep enough to break his fall, and he struggles to the surface, coughing. He feels himself being carried along by the rough water, and the cold numbs the pain in his leg a little. It's now light enough for him to make out some of his surroundings, and he can see the towering wall of granite that he went over on his bike. There's no chance of him getting back up there, and he wouldn't want to either because that's the direction his pursuers will be coming from. He must try to reach the other side. In desperation, he begins to swim. His leg hurts so much that he can't move it, but he pulls strongly with his arms, and slowly but surely, the other side comes closer. It has grown lighter still, and he can see more of the shore he's headed for, but swimming is increasingly difficult. The water is cold, and his clothes feel as heavy as lead. He doesn't dare to abandon his coat. He will desperately need it if he reaches the other side.

"Look there! Look there!" One of the men standing at the side door with night vision goggles is pointing down excitedly. The other man turns his binoculars in the direction indicated. They're flying over a raging torrent and there, against a large rock, is the mutilated carcass of the bike. They tell the pilot to hover, and the pilot and co-pilot also look down at the icy depths. It's now so light that the bike can be seen with the naked eye. The pilot spots it and points it out to his co-pilot. The bike has been wrecked by its collision with the boulder, the front fork protruding upward at an unnatural angle.

The men with the night-vision goggles are now looking in the water and along the shore, but they can't see a body anywhere.

"He must have been swept away by the current," says the co-pilot.

"Would he have survived the fall?" the pilot wonders.

"Depends how deep the water is here," replies his colleague, "you can't tell from the air." The helicopter pilot puts on the spotlight so that the river is illuminated across its full width and then they slowly follow the flow looking for a head sticking up out of the swirling water. The river rushes past boulders, and the co-pilot shudders. You get cold just by looking at it. What it would feel like to be in it, he doesn't like to imagine.

Not pleasant. Mortimer knows all about it. With his teeth tightly clenched, he is still struggling against the flow, and it's a battle he seems to be losing. Yet his hardened body does not give up the battle, and his strong will is even further from defeat. A grim determination has taken possession of him, a certain doggedness that has helped him out more than once in the past. It's this mentality that put him at the top of his empire. Mechanically he pulls his arms through the icy water, ignoring the pain and the cold. He sees only the other side, his way to freedom. Then suddenly, he hears the heavy beating of the rotors of the helicopter. They are back on his tail! If he looks to the side, he can see the helicopter silhouetted against the dark morning sky. The brilliant spotlight casts a wide circle of light over the river. A circle of light which is slowly approaching. If he comes into that circle, they will open fire on him. He moves his arms more quickly through the water. He has to get to the other side! He kicks hard with his good leg. The helicopter is getting closer. The turbulence from the enormous rotors is disturbing the water, and the thundering roar of the engine is deafening over the river. The light moves closer; he isn't going to make it across. He fills his lungs with air, and then dives under water. Around him the water is bright blue as the helicopter's light penetrates deep into the river. Is he visible? Is his body showing as a dark spot against the water? Without resisting he lets himself be carried away by the current, every moment expecting to feel the impact of a bullet. Unable to breathe in the icy water, he feels his oxygen levels depleting. Red spots splash like fireworks before his eyes. He must come up, but the water is still clear blue around him. Why don't they shoot? Then suddenly it's dark, and with a few quick strokes, the fugitive surfaces, pulling air into his lungs. Above him the helicopter is still roaring, but it has moved past him. He can see the light inside the belly of the aircraft, and two men at the side door peering down into the water lit by the spotlight. They haven't seen him! New hope! If he reaches the other side, he is free!

The helicopter throbs across the river.

"Would he have drifted this far?" the co-pilot asks. They should have seen him a long time ago.

"Maybe he climbed out of the water," supposes the pilot, but the co-pilot shakes his head.

"You'd never succeed in reaching the shore in such fast flowing water."

Below them the river is narrowing, and the water flows even faster. They follow the flow for another few hundred yards, and then it suddenly disappears down a yawning black hole. The pilot flies a short way on and then swings round and redirects the spotlight. It illuminates a waterfall plunging at least a hundred feet down and crashing onto rocks at the bottom. "I think we've seen enough," the pilot says soberly, "nobody survives a fall like that. Let's head back, boys!" He pulls the helicopter up and heads back to the airstrip at the old mine.

The other side is just a few yards away, but it's becoming more difficult to swim. The flow is stronger, and Mortimer is growing weaker. The current is still carrying him along, and although he tries to turn his body so that he is driven closer to shore, his limbs are beginning to stiffen from the cold. Suddenly, he hears a faint rumble in the distance. For a moment, he thinks the helicopter's coming back, but then the truth suddenly dawns on him. A waterfall! By the sound of it, it's a big one as well. The river is getting wilder, and the water foams over large boulders emerging from the depths. With difficulty Mortimer steers away from them as the menacing rumble swells. Another moment and he will be washed over the edge. Another large boulder confronts him slanting into the current, and this time he uses all his strength to slide his body on to it. A moment of reprieve! He claws his fingers around the top and works his way up until he can see over the top of the stone. The view is not encouraging. Sixty feet away the river disappears into nothing. In the dim morning light he can see a landscape of mountains, unapproachable cliffs as far as the eye can see. If the river plunges over a cliff like that, he wouldn't bet a penny for his life. How is he going to get safely off this rock? With great effort he works his way up the stone until he is sitting shivering on the top. Just a few feet away is another boulder. If he could reach that one, he could clamber up the bank, but a jump of a yard is a long way when you can only use one leg to push off. Slowly the gang leader stands upright and calculates his chances. His coat is heavy with water, he has to get rid of it. He pulls the zipper down and strips the waterlogged clothing from his body. Folding the jacket into a wet ball, he throws it towards the shore. The garment unfolds in the air, and Mortimer watches anxiously.

If it doesn't reach the shore, he's lost — without a coat, he can't keep warm. The jacket rotates through the air and then, to his great relief, it lands safely on the shore. He concentrates on the other boulder where the water has made the surface slippery, and then with a loud roar, he takes the jump. The rock comes closer, and his foot touches the surface and then slips away! He claws at it desperately as his body slides down the stone, and then he plunges into the water. Sharp pain shoots through his injured leg, but his hands are still clinging to a ledge on the rock. The current drags at his body as if wet hands were pulling him into the depths. With a clenched jaw he hoists his body out of the water again and struggles on to the top of the stone.

Another big jump, and he's made it! He is on the shore! The sun rises, and he sees the long shadow of his body stretching out towards the waterfall, but shadows don't fall and neither will Mortimer. He picks up his sodden coat, squeezes his arms into it and limps to the edge of the waterfall. He is startled by its depth. The thundering river plunges down breaking on the peaks of the rocks below. Shuddering, he sticks his numb fingers into his pockets and feels his lighter there. Fire! He must get somewhere warm as soon as possible, or he will become hypothermic. He looks out across the river once more. It bends to the right, and he assumes the sea lies in that direction. If he went that way, it's likely that he could reach civilization. The terrain is far too steep, and he is forced to turn left, into the wilderness, without food and without any equipment — with nothing in fact, but the clothes he is wearing and a lighter. Furious, he squeezes his hands into fists and grinds his teeth.

"When I get out of here, I will have my revenge!" he hisses.

Four days later, he stumbles through the wilderness, emaciated and ashen. He's torn a strip from his shirt and tied it around his calf to cover over the smelly, inflamed wound. He stares blankly ahead, his eyes hollow in his face.

"De Wolff," he gasps, "professor de Wolff! Your wife and your children! And that miserable radioman! I'll get you! I will crush you," he drops to one knee, "crush you like cockroaches!"

End of Preview

CHESS IN THE WILDERNESS
De Wolff Adventure Series volume 2

A fast-paced roller-coaster suspense for teens set in the Canadian Rocky Mountains which continues the action where *The Vaults of the Titanic* left off.

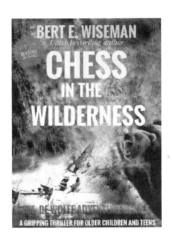

A revenge-seeking criminal. A wild chess game. A plane crash. An unforgiving wilderness. Bears. Dangerous caves. Criminal gangsters watching every move intently.

Willem de Wolff, the Dutch world-renowned history professor, and his wife and children are taken hostage and forced to play a life and death game of chess. They must counteract before they are taken out one by one. A relentless and determined fight for survival that tests the family bond.

Mortimer flees from his criminal hideout in Ungava Bay and narrowly survives a gruelling journey through the wilderness. His plans having been sabotaged and his operations hideout exposed, Mortimer is eager to have the de Wolffs and Andy Howard pay back in equal measure. His growing anger towards them leads him to concoct an evil plan to lure the professor and his family to the rugged north-west of Canada. As a keen chess player, he leaves nothing to chance. Using a plane crash, the unforgiving wilderness, bears, dangerous caves, as well as criminal gangsters to keep an eye on them, his hostages become pieces in a life and death game of chess. Will the pawns be able to defeat the gangster king before they are taken out one by one?

The ever-present tension and action narrated in present tense will keep you on the edge of your seat as you immerse yourself into this survival fiction for teenagers.

AUTHOR'S NOTE

THANK YOU so much for reading my suspense thriller for teens, '**The Vaults of the Titanic**'! Now that you've finished this story, I would greatly appreciate a review on Amazon – please be a super trouper and spare a few minutes to let me know your thoughts on this book – I will personally take the time to read what you  write. Your reviews really do help other readers to discover my writing.

Please say hello via my Facebook author page at www.facebook.com/BertWisemanBooks when you're in the neck of the woods on social media.

Don't miss a beat -- keep up-to-date with news of future books and giveaways -- subscribe to our newsletter or get in touch via the Contact Us form on my website, www.bertwisemanbooks.com. I would love to hear your comments and suggestions.

If you've enjoyed meeting the de Wolff family and want to know what great adventure they're on next, check out the other suspense thrillers for teens in the de Wolff Adventure Series. You can read more about them over the next few pages.

Warm wishes to you all,

Bert

bert*wise*man

OTHER TITLES

Don't miss the other books in the de Wolff adventure series! Let your imagination immerse you into the depth of mystery, action and adventure as you discover more survival fiction for teenagers and older children by the Dutch best-selling author Bert Wiersema, known internationally as

BERT E. WISEMAN

Although occasionally the reading experience may be enhanced by reading previous installments, all of the books in the series make great standalone reads.

CHESS IN THE WILDERNESS

De Wolff Adventure Series volume 2

A fast-paced roller-coaster suspense for teens set in the
Canadian Rocky Mountains which continues the action where
The Vaults of the Titanic left off.

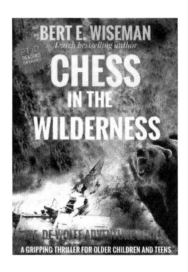

**A revenge-seeking criminal. A wild chess game. A plane crash. An
unforgiving wilderness. Bears. Dangerous caves. Criminal
gangsters watching every move intently.**

Willem de Wolff, the Dutch world-renowned history professor, and his wife and children are taken hostage and forced to play a life and death game of chess. They must counteract before they are taken out one by one. A relentless and determined fight for survival that tests the family bond.

Mortimer flees from his criminal hideout in Ungava Bay and narrowly survives a gruelling journey through the wilderness. His plans having been sabotaged and his operations hideout exposed, Mortimer is eager to have the de Wolffs and Andy Howard pay back in equal measure. His growing anger towards them leads him to concoct an evil plan to lure the professor and his family to the rugged north-west of Canada. As a keen chess player, he leaves nothing to chance. Using a plane crash, the unforgiving wilderness, bears, dangerous caves, as well as criminal gangsters to keep an eye on them, his hostages become pieces in a life and death game of chess. Will the pawns be able to defeat the gangster king before they are taken out one by one? The ever-present tension and action narrated in present tense will keep you on the edge of your seat as you immerse yourself into this survival fiction for teenagers.

Available now on Amazon! amazon

SACRIFICIAL STONE
De Wolff Adventure Series volume 3

A fast-paced mystery and suspense thriller for teens and older children that reads in one breath.

Professor de Wolff, the renowned historian, is invited by Count Francois de Langlebourg to his castle in the French Alps to search for the diaries of St. Bernard of Menthon. Gradually, the de Wolff family discover that there is more to Sir de Langlebourg than meets the eye. The castle is guarded by bodyguards and bloodhounds, and the story soon turns into a nightmare. The diaries refer to a mysterious sacrificial stone in the mountains. Why does the count desperately want to find that stone? Why does an old monk roam around with a shotgun at night on the mountain pass? What is the mysterious tomb in the castle? What secrets are hiding in the ancient monastery of St. Bernard? The de Wolffs become embroiled in a dangerous cat and mouse game.

Expected publication date: December 2017

REVENGE IN NORMANDY
De Wolff Adventure Series volume 4

A fast-paced suspense for teens and older children that will keep you on the edge of your seat.

The wealthy billionaire Hudson Sterling invites the de Wolff family to commemorate D-Day in Normandy. It should be a great package holiday. At the same time, a long-kept family secret is revealed to a brother and sister in Germany. They also leave for France, but with a lot less pleasant plans. During their holiday, the de Wolffs witness an attack on an old resistance fighter. Why would anyone want to murder an old war hero? Unintentionally, the de Wolffs end up in an extortion case. In addition, a mysterious assassin is also assigned to the case. It's a wild chase as the stakes are incredibly high. Will Jessica, Bob and Eric be able to prevent the commemoration of the invasion turning into a bloodbath?

Expected publication date: January 2018

THE OMEGA SHELTER
De Wolff Adventure Series volume 5

A survival fiction for teenagers and older children packed with action and adventure that will keep you guessing.

Sniper Chagall wants revenge after the events in Normandy. A nighttime burglary, mysterious shootings, and a very threatening phone call prompt professor de Wolff and his family to seek police protection. A French secret agent is assigned to bring the de Wolffs to safety. They will be temporarily housed in a safe house for agents — a top secret location called the Omega shelter — but the de Wolffs are far from safe. The road to the shelter appears fraught with danger. Gradually, Jessica, Bob, Eric and their parents find out that they are used as bait in an evil conspiracy. The wildly exciting climax takes place in the Omega shelter where nothing is what it seems and where no one is to be trusted. A thrilling story with countless unexpected plot twists. A must read!

Expected publication date: 2018

Made in the USA
Lexington, KY
15 December 2019

58589000R00192